Schofield's Dilemma

Fatally wounded in the midst of battle, a Union soldier's dying wish was for Jack Schofield to find his heir, to pass over the deeds to a farm in Credence Creek. The task seemed simple, but little did Jack know that his own life would be in danger, as he became deeply involved in a string of complex events.

Threatened by the ominous Rawlson clan, the object of unwanted attention from the crooked president of the Silver Bucket Mining Company and under pressure to help a marshal who seems destined to be killed, Jack finds himself sitting on a powder keg waiting to explode. Unless a miracle happened, it looked as if Jack was destined for an early trip to Boot Hill!

Schofield's Dilemma

SKEETER DODDS

A Black Horse Western

ROBERT HALE · LONDON

© James O'Brien 2003
First published in Great Britain 2003

ISBN 0 7090 7195 7

Robert Hale Limited
Clerkenwell House
Clerkenwell Green
London EC1R 0HT

Typeset by
Derek Doyle & Associates, Liverpool.
Printed and bound in Great Britain by
Antony Rowe Limited, Wiltshire

ONE

'You string that wire and there'll be hell to pay, mister!'

Jack Schofield paused in digging the hole he was preparing for the first pole of a long line, and looked at the silver-haired man who had so angrily addressed him, and whose ruddy features were even more flushed than normal by his temper.

'That a threat, Rawlson?' Schofield asked in his quietly spoken way, his blue eyes hinting at anger.

'No, it ain't, Schofield. . . .'

Schofield looked beyond Charles Rawlson to the younger man astride a feisty black stallion. There was no denying whose seed had produced Spence Rawlson, Charles Rawlson's only son and heir. The younger man had the same hooded grey eyes and slant of jawline, but Spence Rawlson's face had become fleshy with soft living; mean, too, whereas Charles Rawlson's face had all the char-

5

acter and blemishes of a man who had fought the wilderness, and two- and four-legged enemies to build the Rawlson ranch in to the empire it had become.

'That's a promise,' Spence Rawlson growled, and then added vehemently, 'And that'll be Mr Rawlson to you, sodbuster!'

Jack Schofield, a man slow to anger, having seen the futility and carnage of bad blood during the Civil War, was straining at the leash now. His narrowed eyes smouldered. 'I'm not looking for trouble,' he said. 'I'm only protecting my fields from the trampling of Rawlson cows. Which I figure I have a right to do.'

Charles Rawlson said, not for the first time, 'This is not farming country, Schofield. Grass country like this is for cows.'

'And cows only,' added Spence Rawlson, threateningly. 'There's no place here for sodbusters. Sooner you pack up and leave, Schofield, the healthier it'll be for you.'

The glare of Jack Schofield's full attention rested on Spence Rawlson. 'My land is mine to do with as I please,' he said. 'And I don't take kindly to threats, young feller.'

Chancey Grimes, Spence Rawlson's guardian angel when the trouble the rancher's son stirred proved too potent to handle, piped up, 'Well, way I figure, Schofield here has done us a favour . . .'

'Favour?' Spence Rawlson yelped. 'Have you

been supping that mountain man's juice again, Chancey?'

'I ain't finished, Spence,' Grimes whined in his peculiarly pitched voice, only half of which had made the leap from boy to man. 'The sodbuster turning the land will make it easier for us to bury him when the time comes.' He sniggered. 'Which will be pretty soon, I reckon.'

Sneering, Spence Rawlson said, 'You know, Chancey. You're not as godawful dumb as you look.'

'I have my moments, Spence,' Grimes cackled, showing a gap in his teeth punched out by a bar-room brawler's fist which, in a strange sort of way, added an innocence to an otherwise hardcase's dial.

'Yeah,' Spence Rawlson flung back in banter, 'most of them upstairs in the Baldy Critter saloon with that lard-ass, Mollie Flanagan.'

Chancey Grimes sighed. 'I tell ya, Spence. Cuddlin' up to Mollie keeps me young. Kinda like bustin' a mustang, ya know.'

Spence Rawlson chuckled. 'One of these days the strain will kill you, Chancey.'

'Well, a man's gotta go some time, Spence.' Grimes sighed contentedly. 'And when I go, I'd like nothin' better than to go pleasurin' Mollie Flanagan.'

'Shut up the both of you!' Charles Rawlson ordered fierily. Rawlson, a Bible-reading man, did not hold with, or condone lewdness of speech or action. He returned his gaze to Jack Schofield. 'My offer still stands, Schofield.'

'As does my refusal,' Jack Schofield replied.

Charles Rawlson laboured dangerously for breath. In the short time since Schofield had arrived in the valley, he had seen a stark change in the rancher's health. He seemed to be a man under pressure; a lot more pressure than was possible from Rawlson's disagreement with him, Scholfield reckoned.

'If you string wire, you'll cut off access for my cows to the south meadow water—'

'There's plenty of water to the north of the range,' Schofield interjected.

'Water, which in a short time,' Rawlson reminded Schofield, 'will not be fit for cattle to drink.'

Jack Schofield said, uncompromisingly, 'You've got plans you can change, Rawlson,' and added critically, 'You don't have to spoil that water for yourself, or your neighbours.'

'You expect me to leave all that silver lying in those hills of mine?' Charles Rawlson barked.

'The way I see it,' Schofield drawled, his tone even more uncompromising, 'you've got no right to spoil your neighbours' range by dirtying their water. Nor have you a right to bully me in to replacing the water you'll spoil by mining that silver.'

Charles Rawlson threatened. 'I'll be needing water, Schofield. I aim to have it.'

Jack Schofield's gaze went to the fertile fields, soon to be ploughed. 'Can't see how you can have it, Rawlson,' he said. 'Planting crops to have them trampled by your cows, isn't my idea of good business.'

Desperate, the rancher upped his offer. 'I'll raise my buy-out price by twenty-five per cent.'

'Pa,' Spence Rawlson whined. 'You're throwing 'way good money.'

Tempestuously, the rancher retorted, 'Until Gabriel's horn blows, it's my damn money to do what I like with, Spence! Well?' he hounded Schofield. Taking Schofield's silence as an acceptance of his offer, the rancher continued, 'I'll ride straight to town, get the papers drawn up and the money in a sack.'

The rancher was climbing on board his horse when Schofield said, 'I'm staying put, Rawlson.'

A rage bordering on apoplexy gripped Charles Rawlson. 'I've been more than fair and generous with you, Schofield.'

'Don't deny it,' Schofield agreed. 'Thing is, the offer isn't mine to accept or reject.'

'Not yours to . . . ?' Charles Rawlson exploded. 'What devil's game are you playing at, Schofield?'

Spence Rawlson's hand dropped to his gun.

'On your say-so, we can fix this right here and now, Pa,' he panted eagerly.

'Sure thing, Mr Rawlson, sir,' Chancey Grimes chimed in. 'You just give the nod.'

Jack Schofield could see the devil prod the rancher. His desperation made him an easy target for temptation. Schofield reached inside a hollowed out tree-trunk, and drew the rifle he had hidden there for just such an emergency. He levelled the rifle on Spence Rawlson. He promised:

'Start anything, and I'll kill your boy first, Rawlson.'

'Don't listen, Pa,' Spence said cockily. 'I'm fast enough to take him, even toting a primed rifle.'

Chancey Grimes had gone pale about the gills, and began surreptiously to edge his horse out of range from behind Spence Rawlson.

'Stay right where you are, Grimes,' Jack Schofield ordered. He turned to Charles Rawlson, his face grimly determined. 'I mean what I say, if you don't rein in this foolishness.'

Bucking for a fight, Spence Rawlson urged his father, 'Don't pay no heed, Pa. There's three of us, and only one of him.'

'Your boy first,' Schofield chillingly reminded Charles Rawlson.

Seething, the rancher declared, 'You've got the upper hand this time, Schofield.' He pointed to the hollow tree-trunk. 'Good ruse. Really clever. The thing with tricks is, that they only work once.' He mounted up. 'I've tried to do things fairly with you, Schofield, and it's wasted both our time.' He swung his horse about. Holding the reins taut, he warned, 'Next time I'll come prepared. I aim to have my way.'

'I reckon you do at that, Rawlson,' Schofield drawled. 'But if you want to be really fair, you'll let me get on with my business, and you yours, sir. I surely hope that, on reflection, that's the way it'll be.'

'Don't know what this nonsense about you not being able to accept my offer is, Schofield,' the rancher stated grimly. 'Think hard. If you change your mind, drop by the ranch in the next day or two.'

'I won't be dropping by,' Schofield said.

Spence Rawlson glowered. 'He's trouble, Pa. I say settle this now.'

The rancher's son flicked his right wrist, and a stiletto flashed from his sleeve. It whizzed past Schofield. The only thing that saved him from certain death was the untimely bucking of Spence Rawlson's horse, unnerved by the crackling tension in the air.

Incensed by Spence Rawlson's treachery, Jack Schofield's finger curled round the rifle's trigger. On seeing his Grim Reaper mood, the rancher's son blanched.

'Don't,' Charles Rawlson cried out.

'I have every damn right,' Schofield flung back. Rawlson glared at his son with a mixture of anger and disappointment. 'Yes, you have,' he conceded. 'But I'm begging you, Schofield.'

Heeding Charles Rawlson's anguished plea, Jack Schofield's finger eased back on the trigger. He told Spence Rawlson, 'Get out of my sight, before I change my mind.'

Off the hook, Spence Rawlson's cockiness flashed back. But his father ordered:

'Clear out, Spence. Now!'

Smouldering, the rancher's son grudgingly obeyed. Chancey Grimes took off after him. Charles Rawlson delayed a moment.

'I thank you for the mercy you've shown, Schofield.' Then, 'You say my offer isn't yours to accept or reject. How come?'

Jack Schofield took a parchment from his pocket. 'This,' he said, 'is the deed to this property, Rawlson. It was pressed into my hand by a dying Union soldier. His final words to me were: "Find Charlie . . . Inheritance. I've put out word and I'm waiting. As soon as I can, I aim to hand over this deed. So, you see, even if I wanted to take your offer, Rawlson. I couldn't.'

'Not much to go on,' the rancher sensibly opined. 'Likely you'll never find this – *Charlie.*'

'Maybe. But I've got to keep trying for five years.'

'Five years?'

'After that, with the soldier's blessing, if my efforts to find Charlie are honest, this farm is mine.'

'You know, Schofield,' the rancher said, 'we're in one hell of a bind here.'

He galloped off at an angry clip.

'That we surely are, Rawlson,' Jack Schofield muttered. 'That we surely are.'

He returned to the task of erecting the poles on which he would string barbed wire, knowing full well that stringing the wire would fill his cup with trouble to overflowing.

TWO

In the stillness which followed Charles Rawlson's fiery departure, the rustle of a bush sounded like thunder to Jack Schofield's ears. The crack of a trod-on twig put Schofield's watcher directly behind him, in a stand of pine. He did not doubt his ears. Years of stealthily making his way through Union lines had finely tuned his hearing. Schofield put down the rifle he held with an easy casualness, hoping to give the lurker the impression that he was unaware of his presence. He had unavoidably tensed, the way a man does when under an unknown and unquantifiable threat. However, he hoped that his tension had not been communicated to his visitor. He began to scoop out the earth from the hole he had been digging when Charles Rawlson had ridden up, as if that was the only concern he had. But he remained ready for action; ready to dive for the rifle, should he need to. His problem was, that with his back turned to the

14

interloper, he'd have to depend solely on instincts
honed during the war.

He waited.

The next move was down to the watcher.

Spence Rawlson's anger lasted all the way back to
the Rawlson ranch, and even sharpened some. He
stormed into the ranch house, and headed
straight for his father's study. He grabbed a bottle
of whiskey and threw himself into a wingback
chair, one of a pair either side of the fireplace.
Defiantly, he planted his boots on the desk, disre-
garding the damage the spurs would do to the
highly polished surface. He threw aside the drink-
ing-glass he had brought with him from the
drinks cabinet, which his father had shipped in
all the way from Paris, France, and slugged
directly from the bottle, knowing well that such
crudeness of manners would infuriate the old
man when he arrived, which was going to be any
second now, since his footsteps were coming along
the hall to the study.

Charles Rawlson stood in the study door, fuming
on seeing Spence's disrespectful pose. He stormed
across the study and grabbed the bottle of whiskey.
Then he swept Spence's legs off the desk. His anger
reached a peak on seeing the meandering scrawl
his son's spurs left on the desktop.

Spence Rawlson sprang to his feet, his anger
every bit as keen as his father's.

'Don't treat me like a kid, Pa,' he growled. 'Because I'm not. I'm twenty-two years old. I'm a grown man, dammit!'

Charles Rawlson snorted. 'Some men can be all of seventy, and still not grown.' Suddenly weary, his anger spent, the rancher sighed. 'I reckon you fit into that category, Spence.'

Spence Rawlson strode angrily to the door. 'You might be willing to sit back and let Schofield destroy this ranch, Pa. But I'm not!'

Charles Rawlson went to the study door to call after his son, who was continuing his angry stride along the hall. 'Spence.' The young man kept walking. 'You hold up right now, boy!' Rawlson ordered fierily.

Spence Rawlson checked his stride. He hadn't often seen his father in a rage, but when he had it was a sight to behold. Charles Rawlson came along the hall to stand toe to toe with his son.

'I don't have the answer to Jack Schofield's antics, yet,' he said. 'But of one thing you can be sure, Spence. I'm not going to allow him to spoke our wheels.'

'That,' Spence Rawlson growled, 'makes two of us, Pa.'

Jack Schofield's tension eased. His watcher was creeping away. The rustle of leaves, a brush with undergrowth, another snapping twig, more distant. Who was it? A back-up Rawlson hand? Schofield could believe that Spence Rawlson would be so underhanded, but, he figured, not Charles Rawlson. Rawlson senior had the jib of a man who faced up to his opponents fair and square. Maybe a Rawlson hand who had ambitions to put himself in Spence Rawlson's good books by solving a thorny problem for him?

Whoever, Jack Schofield did not like a creeper.

Schofield had options. He could let the lurker sneak away. Or he could confront him. He decided on the latter. Grabbing his rifle, he turned and shot into the trees where he reckoned the lurker was. His bullet buzzed a tree and bark fanned out. A screech emanated from the pines. A woman danced in to the open, rubbing her backside.

'What did you do that for, mister?' she yelped. 'That tree-bark near ruined my best feature.'

Schofield, though surprised that the interloper was a woman, still barked, 'Drop the rifle.' He'd known women who had been by far more vicious killers than men. This one did not seem the killer type, but he wasn't taking any chances.

'I don't mean you no harm, mister,' the pert blonde whined.

'Well, if you drop that rifle you won't be able to do me any,' Schofield reasoned. 'Who are you?'

'Charlotte Scott. Don't you trust me?' the woman asked, surprise animating her blue eyes.

'I'd be a fool to trust a creeper, Charlotte,' Schofield snapped.

'Creeper?' The woman's tone was one of righteous indignation. 'And folk round here call me
Lotte.'

'Creeper. That's what you are,' Schofield stated
bluntly. 'What else would you call a skulker
hiding in the trees?'

'Skulker?' the blonde's indignation notched up.

'Drop the rifle,' Jack Schofield repeated. 'Now!'

Reluctantly, the woman flung the rifle from her.
'Satisfied?'

'No. Not until you tell me what you were planning on doing. And who you were planning on
doing it for? Spence Rawlson, maybe?'

'Spence Rawlson?' the woman scoffed. 'You
haven't been around here long, have you, mister?
Because if you had been, you'd know that Lotte
Scott and Spence Rawlson hate each other's guts.'

'That a fact?'

'That's a fact!'

'So, why were you lurking?' Schofield persisted.

'I thought you might be needing some help. It
was looking that way.'

'Why would you want to help me?' Jack
Schofield questioned. 'We've never even met,
young lady.'

'Well, if you hate the Rawlsons, that makes you
Lotte Scott's friend. Simple as that.'

Schofield stated, 'I don't hate the Rawlsons,
Miss Scott.'

'You should.'

'Why?'

'Well,' Lotte said, flustered, 'you just should. They're trying to run you off, aren't they? You must be loco, of course . . .'

'You're entitled to your opinion,' Schofield drawled, secretly admiring Lotte Scott's feistiness.

'. . . wanting to use a plough on cow range. No sodbuster's ever got to set down roots in these parts. Why, over Clancyville way, which isn't much further than a good spit from here, only last week they strung up a farmer.'

'Isn't there any law around here?'

'Sure there's law.'

'The three monkeys kind of law?'

'Huh?' Lotte Scott's brow furrowed in puzzlement.

'The kind of law that sees nothing. Hears nothing. Says nothing.'

Lotte's cheeks flushed with anger. 'I'll have you know that, in Hal Bateman, Credence Creek's got the finest darn marshal who ever pinned on a star.'

'Bateman? Tall? Skinny as a starved crow kind of fella?'

'Slim,' Lotte rebuked. 'Not skinny. Hal's muscles are budding more every day.'

Jack Schofield smiled. 'Seems to me that you're kind of sweet on this Marshal Bateman, young lady.'

Lotte Scott's blush deepened to scarlet. 'None of your business, how I feel about Hal Bateman. Now, if you don't mind, I'll be getting along.'

Schofield said, 'Jack Schofield's my handle, Lotte. He invited, 'Step inside the house. I was just about to brew fresh coffee.' Lotte shrugged indecisively. 'There's a cold wind coming up. Hot coffee will keep out the chill on the ride back to town.'

'Well . . .'

Mischievously, Schofield said, 'Wouldn't want those lips to turn blue. Why, Hal Bateman might just want to warm them up.'

Lotte Scott let out a yelp of raucous laughter. 'You reckon? Then, no disrespect, Mr Schofield. But you can keep your darn coffee.' She whistled and a horse came from the trees. She picked up her rifle and climbed on board the mare. Before she departed, Lotte warned solemnly, 'You be real careful of those Rawlsons. Especially Spence Rawlson. That one's a viper.'

'Appreciate the advice, Lotte.'

'You're surely welcome to it, Mr Schofield.'

'That'll be Jack, Lotte.'

Shaking her head, she said, 'Sodbusting in cow country? Jack, you don't seem to have much sense in that skull of yours.'

'Tell the marshal I'll drop by in a day or two,' he called after her. 'Pay my respects.'

'Make it an evening call,' she shouted.

'Why an evening call?'

'Come and see me at the Baldy Critter.'

'The saloon?'

'Finest in Credence Creek.'

'You're a—'

Schofield's surprised question was cut short by Lotte Scott's interruption.

'I'm a warbler, Jack.'

As Lotte Scott charged into the distance, she left Jack Schofield scratching his black thatch. 'Well, I'll be . . .' he murmured.

THREE

Jack Schofield was not a saloon drinking man, preferring his brew by the flames of a leaping log fire in homely surroundings. The bawdy environs of a saloon had never appealed to him. He supposed that his dislike of saloons and their bawdy goings-on was the result of his Quaker upbringing by Jethro Schofield, his adoptive father. He had, it seemed, little if any of his natural father in him. He had heard many stories of the famous, or infamous, Frank Scully; his standing depended on the Frank Scully you had crossed paths with. A few, but only a few, said that he was a good man. Most said he was a vagabond and a rogue. And some said he was a black-hearted killer. The truth, as always, lay some-where in between. However, all men agreed that Frank *King of Hearts* Scully, was a gambler, a womanizer, a bank-robber, and a horse-thief – this last being the crime he had been strung up for when his luck had finally run out.

Jack was seven years old, when his mother had died from the stress and hard times she had endured with a man who treated her worse than his horse, and broke her heart with a frequency that stole her will to fight her illness, preferring instead to welcome the Grim Reaper. Hers had been a life of tent-towns and mining-camps where, when Frank Scully ran short of money to back yet another winning hand (they were all winning hands), he had no qualms about hiring his wife out to fund his gambling and alcohol sickness. When Mary Scully died in a grubby hotel room, exhausted by yet another client, the latest in a long line since her husband had been strung up, Jack Scully had been sitting quietly in the hotel foyer, used to a routine which had become the norm for him.

Jethro Schofield, a Christian and non-judgemental man, who had come to town to take on supplies for the trek to a new homestead in Tennessee, had stepped in to say the words over Mary Scully's grave when the righteous had shunned the sinner, many of whom had had no objections to enjoying her when she'd been alive.

'What about the boy?' the town marshal had asked Schofield after the funeral.

'I'm sure some Christian soul will take him in, Marshal,' had been Jethro Schofield's response.

The marshal had scoffed. 'A whore's spit. Ain't likely. A man's got to protect his own against being tainted, I say.'

Schofield had been truly shocked by the lawman's unChristian views. 'He's just a boy. With the right caring he'll be a fine citizen.'

'You think so?' the marshal had said, smug that he had led Jethro Schofield in to the trap he had so carefully set for him. 'Then I guess you'd be the best man to see that that happens, mister.'

Later, when Jack was fifteen, the man who had lovingly cared for him and given him his name, took him aside and explained the events of that day eight years previously. 'I've prayed long and hard for the Lord's forgiveness for my thoughts on that day,' he had frankly told Jack. 'For my small-mindedness at a time when the Lord was calling on me to be his true disciple.' On that early summer day, with soft winds blowing through the orchard he had nurtured at his homestead, Jethro Schofield had wept. 'I almost didn't take you with me, Jack. Like the marshal that day, I too, feared mixing you with Nathan and Jude, my own flesh and blood. I almost hadn't the faith in our Lord Jesus, to trust in his kind and caring hands to make things right, as he surely has.'

It meant the world to Jack Schofield that day when, cradling him in his arms, his adoptive father had held him and had told him:

'You've been a son to be truly proud of, Jack.

And I thank God for the blessing and privilege of having been given the opportunity to rear and mould you as my own.'

Jack Schofield had been obedient to his adoptive father's will in all matters, except one; that one matter had caused a bitter rift in their relationship which, at some future date, when he mustered the courage to return and face Jethro Schofield, an old man now, Jack hoped to mend. That rift had been brought about by his wearing the grey of the Confederacy.

'But you're a Quaker, Jack,' his adoptive father had pleaded with him on that bleak afternoon, the last they had spent in each other's company. 'Your gospel and creed is one of peace and goodwill to all men. It's for God to judge right and wrong, Jack. And it's our job to pray that men will understand the Lord's love for all men. Black, white, blue and grey.'

Jack had seen the coming conflict differently. He saw it as his duty to bear arms with his fellow Southerners, and that he should not stand aside. Jack Schofield believed that to be part of the future, a man had to choose a side in the present.

Before he rode away, Jack Schofield had asked for Jethro Schofield's forgiveness.

'It is not my place to judge you, Jack,' he'd said. 'However, going against my wishes, which I truly believe are those of our Lord Jesus, pains me to the point of, God forgive me, anger. How long that anger will last, I have no way of knowing, Jack. I will sincerely pray that it will be short-lived.'

From the battlefields of the Civil War, Jack Schofield had written many letters, all of which had gone unanswered.

Now, standing on the threshold of the Baldy Critter saloon, Jack Schofield wondered how critical of his decision to imbibe in a saloon, on a racuous Saturday night, Jethro Schofield would be. He had come to hear Lotte Scott sing, if a single note she warbled could be heard above the din.

The war had robbed him of his innocence, of course, but Jack hoped it had not of his decency, as it had so many men. The bloody and bitter conflict had irrevocably changed most men, brutalizing and hardening them, body and soul. It had instilled in them the doctrine that might was right, and the guns which they had in many cases grown to love, were often used in the melting pot of the West in preference to discussion and dialogue, which had come a poor second to gunfire for fellow Americans during the determination of the future of their great country.

'Why, hello there, stranger.' Jack felt himself dragged into the mêlée by a red-haired saloon dove who was barely of beddable age, but who already had the guile of a woman who knew men's foibles and weaknesses. 'Mine will be Kentucky rye, mister. And later . . .' Her faded blue eyes flicked in the direction of the stairs. She laughed. 'But that'll cost you more than a shot of rye, ya understand?'

Jack stated flatly, 'I'm not here for liquor or women, young lady.'

'Young lady?' A dribbling man at the bar sniggered. 'I bet, Mary Rose, that's the first time any man's called you that.'

The young woman slapped the drunk on the back in bonhomie. 'You can say that again, Larry. Right fellas?' Raucous, leering laughter spread along the length of the bar. The dove returned her attention to Jack Schofield. 'Now, mister,' her tone was hard; her eyes harder still. 'If you don't want to drink and you don't want to bed, what the hell're ya doin' in a saloon?'

'I've come to hear Lotte Scott sing,' Jack told Mary Rose.

'Lotte.' The dove snorted contemptuously. Then her eyes glowed with mischief. She addressed the men gathering round Jack Schofield, as if he were some strange species they'd never set eyes on before. 'Hey, fellas. Mebbe the stranger here thinks that he's goin' to be Lotte's first, just like all you horny old bastards thought you would be.'

A ginger-haired drinker said, 'Mister, if that's the way you're thinking, you can just forget it. What God gave Lotte Scott, she intends to return intact.'

Laughter, as swift as wildfire, swept along the bar and beyond as the theory about Jack Schofield's visit was retold, each time, judging by the hike in laughter, more lewdly. An old-timer going from the dregs of one glass to another, opined:

'A clean-cut fella like you might just loosen the screws on Lotte Scott's drawers at that.'

Several men handed their dregs to the old-timer in appreciation of another round of laughter.

Jack Schofield, infuriated not by any comments directed his way, but rather by the cat-calling and snide laughter at Lotte Scott's expense, sunk his fist in the gob of a particularly obnoxious man near him. The blow flattened the man against the bar. With the reflexes of a man used to saloon brawling, the brawny specimen came back at Schofield brandishing the neck of a broken whiskey bottle, its jagged edge sweeping up to plunge into Schofield's neck.

Schofield arched back. The makeshift but deadly weapon flashed past his right cheek. The flickering glint of the candle chandelier above him reflected off the bottle, cold and evil. The man lunged past Schofield, taken on by his own momentum. Schofield added to the man's headlong sprawl by placing his boot on the man's rump. He pitched foward, crashing through several tables. The crowd, not eager to become

involved and draw either man's wrath on their
heads, stepped aside, and a path opened up all the
way to the stairs, against which the man's head
collided with a gut-wrenching thud. He should
have folded – most men would have. But not
Barney Bumstead. The man was a lumberjack,
employed on felling a stand of pine to the south of
Schofield's farm. He had brawn and muscle
aplenty, and Schofield knew that in a straight
slugging contest, he would not stand a chance of
coming out on top. But the lumberjack's beefiness
also slowed his movements. This left him open to
danger from a man of niftier feet and fists like
Jack Schofield.

The crowd, as yet, remained strictly neutral;
folk knew well from past experience that taking
sides so early in a fight could land them in all
sorts of trouble, if their choice proved to be
unwise. So it was best to hold off on cheering for
either contestant, until there were signs of a clear
winner emerging. Then, and only then, would it be
opportune to join the winner's entourage.

Bumstead shook his head until his eyes came
together again, by which time Jack Schofield's
next pile-driver was flying towards his jaw. To the
farmer's surprise, his hammer-blow put only the
merest quiver in the lumberjack's legs. Schofield's
left swung – Bumstead parried. Schofield ducked
under the returning iron fist headed his way, and
it punched air. The farmer came out of his crouch

and landed a gut-cruncher in the lumberjack's belly. But, so taut were Bumstead's stomach muscles, Jack Schofield's balled fist bounced off the tree-feller's midriff, causing him more grief than Bumstead. The lumberjack side-swiped Schofield, and he felt himself sucked into a whirlpool that threatened to pull him under. He flew through the air under the force of Bumstead's blow, which hurtled him over the bar and into the shelves behind, bringing them crashing down. Luckily, if being hit so hard by the lumberjack could be called luck in any shape or form, the momentum of his collision with the wall behind the bar pitched him back on top of the counter, out of harm's way from the shattered glass from the bar mirror and a hundred bottles littering the floor.

Jack Schofield's eyes focused just in time to see Barney Bumstead bearing down on him, maulers in claws to encircle his throat. He used the polished surface of the bar to slide out of the lumberjack's way, and when Bumstead was splayed across the bartop, grabbing air, his target gone, Schofield landed a boot on the side of the tree-feller's head. It was like kicking solid rock, and pain shot along Schofield's leg, numbing it as far as his groin.

Bumstead wiped a dribble of whiskey from his jaw, and glared at Schofield. Now the crowd had decided on the winner, and their whole-hearted support was for Bumstead. So much so, that hands grabbed Schofield and slid him back along the bar to a spine-crushing bearhug which, Jack had no doubt, would snap his spine should he be ensnared in it. On he slid relentlessly, unable to find purchase on the bartop. When he almost did, more hands reached out to keep him on sliding.

Jack Schofield did not regret having started the fight. But he was sure going to regret its outcome.

FOUR

Just as Bumstead's arms encircled Jack Schofield, a bullet tore a chunk out of the floor an inch from the lumberjack's right leg. The spinning splinter of wood shot upwards and caught Bumstead high up on the left thigh. He danced about as if his pockets had caught fire. Enraged by the painful intervention, he flung Schofield from him. Schofield went crashing to the floor, taking a dozen men with him in a cursing, unruly pile. All eyes went to the balcony which ran in a horseshoe above the bar, to where Lotte Scott was standing, toting a smoking pistol.

'Why I bother singing for you so-called gentlemen is a pure wonder to me,' Lotte said. 'Now I don't know what you fellas are barging about,' Lotte pointed the Colt at Schofield and Bumstead, 'and I don't really care. But,' she stated, 'if you want to hear me sing tonight, you'll both shake hands and stop your antics.'

'Ma'am,' Bumstead said, taking a little bow.

'Mr Schofield,' Lotte said. 'Take the man's hand and let that be an end of it.'

Schofield said, getting gingerly off the floor, 'If that's your wish, Lotte.'

'It is.'

'Then . . .'

Jack Schofield held out his hand to shake Barney Bumstead's. It was like putting his hand in a vice. For Lotte Scott's benefit, the lumberjack's smile was beatific. But as he turned his back on her to face Schofield, he told him:

'We've got unfinished business, sodbuster.'

'Barney,' Lotte called out, 'I've got ears that would hear a ghost's footsteps. And I heard what you just said. No more fighting, understood?'

'But, Lotte—'

The warbler cut the lumberjack short. 'No more fisticuffs, I said!'

'Ah, heck, Lotte,' Bumstead groaned.

'Promise me, Barney.'

'I promise, Lotte.'

'Right, then.' Lotte handed the pistol back to the tipsy cowboy from whose holster she had grabbed it a moment before. 'Maestro, if you please.'

The fabulously moustachioed man conducting the saloon ensemble raised his baton, quivered it in the air, and struck up Lotte Scott's introduction. The saloon might have been a church, it became so hushed and reverent. Lotte strode along the balcony towards the curving staircase, every step laced with coal-hot temptation. When she sang, Jack Schofield had never heard such sweetly sung notes before.

Under a silver moon.
With a man like you . . .

Jack Schofield thought for sure that Lotte Scott's gaze was solely for him until, glancing around, he saw that every other man in the Baldy Critter thought exactly the same thing. Lotte had the knack of all great performers, and that was to make each member of her audience special.

Holding hands, doing things we shouldn't do . . .

The saloon erupted into bawdiness. The song grew bolder and bolder in tone until Lotte reached the end of the stairs. She was hoisted on to the bar, where, strutting its length she finished her song, each man there in love with her by then. When the *brouhaha* died down, and Schofield could find a way through the milling crowd, he left. Lotte Scott joined him at the batwings. They left together, Jack Schofield the envy of every man in Credence Creek.

'That fella Schofield musta rocks in his head,'

one imbiber confided to another, 'walking off like that with Lotte. Spence Rawlson will rip his innards out.'

'You reckon Lotte's got an eye for the sodbuster, Jim?' the imbiber's confidant asked. 'Pile of years 'tween them.'

'Don't matter none, Lew,' the other opined. 'Like I said. Spence Rawlson will kill him for sure. Lotte is Spence's prop'ty. Ev'ryone knows that.'

'What 'bout our marshal? Lotte seems keen on him.'

The man called Jim chuckled. 'Lotte's a saloon woman. Takes lotsa 'tention to keep a saloon woman contented. Hal Bateman ain't man 'nuff to tame Lotte Scott.'

'Lotte ain't no saloon woman, like other saloon women!'

The two men quaked at the sight of Barney Bumstead. The lumberjack's scowling gaze settled on Jim. 'Don't reckon you should be sayin' she is.' Bumstead grabbed both men by their shirt fronts, the cloth ripping in his hands. He lifted them effortlessly off their feet. 'If I ever hear you say so again . . .' There was no need to finish his threat. The gossiping pair had seen the condition of other men who had insulted Lotte Scott, after Barney Bumstead had chastised them.

'Not 'nother word will pass my lips, Barney,' Jim vowed.

It was a vow which Jim's partner hurriedly agreed to abide by.

'Walk me home, Jack,' Lotte invited.

'It'll be my pleasure, Lotte. But don't you live in the saloon?'

'I do not,' she replied, indignantly wide-eyed. 'What kind of a girl do you think I am, Jack?'

Schofield cringed under Lotte's angry glare, and then smiled. 'You know, Lotte, if I'm not careful, I could end up spending my time saying sorry to you.'

Her blue-eyed gaze was impish. 'Keeping a man humble, is the best way to keep a man keen, I reckon, Jack.'

'Doesn't that depend on the man?' Schofield speculated. 'All men aren't from the same mould, Lotte.'

Lotte Scott gave Jack Schofield slow and careful consideration.

'You know, Jack,' she said, smiling crookedly, 'you just might have a point there.'

As they strolled on, the object of curious scrutiny, Schofield asked with a sizeable degree of amusement. 'You know a lot about men, Lotte?'

'Only from looking, Jack.' She sighed deeply. 'Only from looking.'

A man who had slipped out of the Baldy Critter, watched from the shadows as Jack Schofield and Lotte Scott strolled along the moon-dappled street to the small clapboard house at the end of Main. When they went inside, he went briskly to his hitched horse and vaulted into the saddle. Then he wheeled the horse at a sharp angle and charged along Main, anxious, and a little gleeful, too, to be the bearer of the news to Spence Rawlson.

'Some supper, Jack?' Lotte asked.

'Don't mind if I do.'

'Ain't going to be much,' she warned. 'Just coffee and some reheated meat pie.'

'Well, Lotte,' Jack Schofield drawled, 'I ain't the picky kind. Never had the cooking skills to grub fancy. And never had the poke to buy fancy. Meat pie will be just fine.'

The hastily prepared meal over with, Schofield sat sipping his coffee, waiting for Lotte to get to the reason why she had invited him back to her house. It had to be an important reason. In a Western town, with its stifling propriety, an invitation such as Lotte Scott had extended to Jack Schofield would do a powerful amount of damage to a woman's reputation. And probably demolish it outright if the invitation were extended into the wee hours.

'You haven't got a lot to say for yourself, Jack,' Lotte said, coming out of a particularly deep stretch of thought.

Schofield put down his coffee cup, took the makings from his vest pocket and rolled a smoke, and leisurely fired it up. He puffed. He let the smoke trickle down his left nostril and watched it drift away.

'I've been waiting for you to give me the reason you invited me here, Lotte,' he said.

'Reason?'

'Yep. I've enjoyed your company, your grub, and your hospitality. Now, I reckon, it's time you said what you want to say, before my hair greys with waiting.'

Put in the spotlight, Lotte shifted uneasily in her chair. 'You're a sharp-witted critter, aren't you, Jack.'

'It's how I'm still sucking air, Lotte.'

Making up her mind, the singer dispensed with the frills and came straight to the point. 'It's Hal – Hal Bateman, Jack . . .'

'Go on,' Schofield urged. 'What about the Marshal?'

Lotte sprang from her seat, frustrated. 'Well, Hal isn't the brighest wick in the store, if you get my drift. . . ?'

'I do.'

'But he's honest and hardworking, and too darn proud of that badge he's toting. Cripes, he believes all that stuff about upholding the law honestly and without favour.'

'What's wrong with that?'

'Nothing. Except when you're in love with the dull wick who believes in it. If Hal keeps stepping on Spence Rawlson's toes, the way he's been doing, he'll surely end up as daisy-fodder. Spence Rawlson is so mean spirited that he'd strike fear in a rattler if he came eye to eye with him!'

'Bateman is a town marshal. What happens out on the range isn't any of his affair. So, why. . . ?' Jack Schofield studied Lotte. 'I see. Spence Rawlson wants first call on your affections. Right?'

Lotte smiled. 'You're no dull wick, Jack.'

'I'm not so sure about that, Lotte. I don't see the problem here. Tell Rawlson to back off. State your preference for Hal Bateman. You're preference is for Bateman, isn't it?'

'Surely is, in bucketfuls.'

'Then—'

'I've told Spence Rawlson a hundred times that I'd rather lie with a darn viper than him. But he says that I don't mean it, and that eventually I'll get sense in my skull and see what a fine catch he is.'

'Don't know how I can help, Lotte,' her guest admitted honestly. Alarmed, he asked, 'You're not looking for a chaperon with a gun, are you?'

Lotte yelped, 'You think I'd want you hanging around when me and Hal are canoodling?'

Exasperated, Schofield said, 'Then what do you think I could do, Lotte?'

'Adopt me, Jack.'

'What!'

'Not like you'd adopt a mite. Kind of as a guardian angel.'

Jack Schofield grinned. 'I'm no angel, Lotte.'

'You're being obtuse, Jack,' Lotte chanted.

'Obwhat?'

'Dumb.'

'Well, why didn't you say so,' Schofield complained, 'instead of spouting hundred-dollar words. Where the hell did you get such words anyway, Lotte?'

'From the people who adopted me.'

'You were adopted?'

'Being adopted isn't mortal sin, Jack,' Lotte retorted sharply, in response to Schofield's surprise, which to Lotte sounded like criticism.

'Me, too.'

'Adopted?'

'Yep.'

Quick as a snake's tongue, Lotte chirped, 'You've got to help me, Jack. Now that we've got so much in common.'

'Hold it right there!' Schofield said, and grabbed his hat from the table. 'Anyone ever tell you that you're a contriving woman, Lotte Scott?' Schofield was at the front door when Lotte caught him up.

'Jack,' she pleaded, contritely. 'Won't you please help Hal?'

His anger draining away, Schofield asked, 'How?'

'By becoming his deputy.'

'Deputy!'

'Yes.' Lotte's face clouded with worry. 'I figure

that a showdown with Spence Rawlson isn't far off. It's a darn wonder that it hasn't come before now. Only the other night, it almost did.'

'How?'

'Spence Rawlson kissed me.'

'It isn't a crime to peck a pretty girl's cheek, Lotte.'

'It wasn't that kind of kiss, Jack. He did it right out there in the street when Hal came to the law office door for a smoke, the way he does late at night when there's a full moon.' Lotte sighed, and hugged herself. 'Hal likes looking at the moon. Gets all spouty when he does. Turn a girl's head in a flash, he would.'

Worry returned to chase away Lotte Scott's dreamy mood.

'Hal's habits are well known,' she explained. 'Spence Rawlson knew exactly what he was doing. He wanted to goad Hal into a gunfight, knowing that Hal wouldn't stand a chance. Hal isn't a gun-handy man, Jack. It would have been plain murder. Nothing else.'

'What stopped the Marshal?'

'Doc Witherspoon. Made such a fuss about any fight being so one-sided as to be downright unjust, Spence Rawlson was forced to back off to save face. But he had a killer's look in his eyes, Jack. The kind of look that seeps out of a black heart and an even blacker soul. He'll steer Hal into another showdown for sure. Soon, too.'

Lotte Scott placed her hand on Jack Schofield's arm, as a daughter might with a loving father.

'Spence Rawlson will find a way to murder Hal Bateman, of that I'm certain.' She pleaded: 'You've got to help him, Jack. You've got to help *me*. That's why I was out at your place today. I was looking for your help then. I hid in the trees when I saw the Rawlsons ride up. And when you flushed me out, I figured it wasn't the right time to ask for favours.' She concluded earnestly: 'But I would have helped, if *you'd* needed help, Jack.'

Jack Schofield was in a hellish bind. Refusing to help the delectable Lotte Scott did not settle well with him. However, getting involved with the Rawlsons more than he already was, would be loco. Once he'd found the soldier's boy and handed over his inheritance, he intended to shake off Credence Creek's dust. Pinning on a star was not in his plans.

Schofield had counted on finding Charlie long before now, but the disruption of war and the town's constantly shifting population made finding him more difficult than he had anticipated. He also had to be certain that he handed over the farm to the right claimant. A couple of shysters had tried to hoodwink him. Finding Charlie, along with getting the farm in to shape, left little time for works of charity, like helping Hal Bateman.

Credence Creek was a drifters' town. Some Western towns were like that: towns where the

population continually changed. Folk drifted in –
folk drifted out. There was no good reason why
they should; Credence Creek was a pleasant
enough place to live. But Western towns, in their
early days of existence, took on a mood that
persisted. If they were drifter towns, then they
remained drifter towns – settler towns remained
settler towns. Credence Creek stood at a junction
between several other towns, which were not
more or less prosperous, but folk thought they
might be. And that *might* made the hills beyond
Credence Creek look greener. The constantly
changing population meant that the town did not
have a history. Folks' memory of people and
events did not extend back very far. The confusion
of war had exacerbated these problems, which
made the whereabouts of Charlie infinitely more
difficult, if not downright impossible to pin down.

Credence Creek had suffered heavily in the
war, losing most of its settled citizens (those who
might have had an inkling who Charlie was), in a
foolish skirmish with Confederate forces who, if
they'd had any sense, would have let the Rebs
sneak past in the night as they had intended to. A
handful of old-timers had survived the skirmish,
but their minds were rambling, and each time
Schofield had spoken to them, he had come away
with a different story – most times with no story
at all. One old-timer had remembered a man
answering to the soldier's description.

'But he didn't have no boy,' the old-timer had adamantly insisted. 'Didn't stay 'round long neither.' Sadly he said, 'No one does, mister.'

The following day when Schofield had gone back to check again on the old-timer's story, he had completely forgotten who Schofield was.

Shackling himself to a deputy's badge to shepherd the ill-equipped Hal Bateman could become a mill-stone round his neck that would prove difficult to shift when he decided to move on. What the hell was a gangling, awkward, clod-footed, slow-gun fella like Bateman wearing a marshal's badge for anyway? The answer, of course, was simple. No one else wanted the job. It paid poorly. Any day could bring trouble in the shape of a drifting gunnie. And Spence Rawlson's continuous trouble-stirring was a thorn that most would not want in their side.

Besides, a good lawman had to care for the town he toted a badge in. And the fact was, Jack Schofield could not care a fig about Credence Creek or its citizens, with one exception, of course – Lotte Scott. And how in tarnation could a looker like Lotte have fallen for a no-consequence fella like Hal Bateman in the first place?

Women were surely a mystery.

Lotte cut in on Schofield's reverie. 'Will you stand with Hal, Jack?' she asked.

Schofield's answer sorely grieved him. 'I've got a plateful of my own trouble, Lotte.'

The singer's shoulders slumped. 'I guess I'll

have to kill Spence Rawlson myself, to protect Hal from his evil machinations.'

Schofield chuckled. 'There you go again with those hundred dollar words.'

'Saul Scott, my adoptive father, was an educated man. A banker.'

'A banker? How come you're a sal . . .' Schofield chewed off his words.

'Saloon singer? The Scotts paid for singing lessons. Ethel Scott thought I'd be an opera singer. Disappointed her something awful when I took to singing ditties. I'm good at singing saloon songs, but no good at all at singing opera. Ethel Scott never forgave me. Saul Scott forbade me to sing saloon songs, and locked me in the cellar when I rebelled. I guess that was the end of my time with the banker and his wife. I was seventeen years old, and they wanted to keep me seven years old. One night Saul forgot to fasten the cellar window, and I escaped.'

'Why did you come here to Credence Creek, Lotte?' Schofield asked.

'No particular reason. I was part of a travelling show that happened to stop here. Liked the feel of the town. Somehow it appealed to me. Kind of homely, I guess. Got a job in the Baldy Critter. And there you have it.'

'Best say goodnight, before the purity league come hammering on the door, Lotte,' Schofield advised.

Jack Schofield had his hand on the door latch when it crashed open. Hal Bateman, his eyes glowing like a mountain cat's with anger, blocked Schofield's path. Bateman's fist flashed. Schofield felt its bony contact on his jaw. Bateman was hardly more than a youngster, with muscles still developing, but such was the fury backing his fist that it staggered Schofield back along the hall. A little more venom, and Jack Schofield's backside would have kissed the ground.

'Hal Bateman,' Lotte rebuked the fuming marshal, 'what on earth do you think you're playing at?'

Bateman's fury was now directed at Lotte. 'Guess I figured you wrong, Lotte Scott.'

'And how would that be?' the singer fierily challenged.

'No respectable woman would leave the saloon with a man and take him to her house the way you did.'

'I didn't take Jack—'

'Jack, huh!' Bateman raged.

'Hal Bateman,' Lotte growled, 'you're as off-beam as a Saturday-night drunk. And behaving worse.'

'He's been here for most of an hour!' Bateman railed.

'That temper of yours is sure to put you in a pine box, if you don't curb it, Hal,' she told him. 'Why, you sparkle faster than a dynamite fuse.'

'With good cause, I reckon,' the marshal flung back.

'Ja . . . Mr Schofield is—'

'What?' Bateman interjected hotly.

'An old friend of my father's,' Lotte lied, and shot Schofield a desperate look for backing. 'Isn't that so, Jack?' To Lotte's way of thinking she had to lie. She could hardly tell the man she loved heart and soul, that she had been pleading with Jack Schofield to mollycoddle him.

Schofield added lie to lie, not liking the idea of getting in deeper to Lotte Scott's contriving, but left with little alternative if he wanted to avoid further ugliness – maybe even gunplay. Because Hal Bateman was surely riled enough to go for the .45 inexpertly hung on his right hip.

'That's so, Marshal,' Jack Schofield said.

Bateman asked suspiciously, 'Then how come he didn't come calling before now, Lotte? And in daylight, too?'

The singer was stumped for an answer. It was left to Schofield to supply one. Because if they had to backtrack and admit now to their lying, the top of Hal Bateman's head was liable to lift right off with fury.

Schofield said, 'Because I was fearful of paying my respects, Marshal . . .'

Schofield had baited the trap. He waited.

'Why?' Bateman asked.

'Because I feared exactly what happened right

now, would happen. I knew Lotte, being the pretty peach she is, would have some jealous sprig who'd go off half-cocked.'

Hal Bateman shuffled. 'Gee, I'm sorry, Lotte.' Then, stridently defensive, he said, 'But I guess too that you've only yourself to blame. What was I to think? You bringing a man home. Damn it, Lotte. It near unhinged my mind, woman.'

Lotte kissed the marshal on the cheek, and his colour rose. He shuffled some more.

'Dang it, Lotte. Smooching should be private.'

Jack Schofield reflected again on what the beautiful Lotte Scott saw in the stringy, gawky-limbed Hal Bateman. But of all the strange things in the world, Schofield reckoned that love and a woman's heart were the strangest of all.

Now that he'd seen the marshal close-up, Jack Schofield could understand Lotte's fears for his survival in any showdown with the agile, quick-handed and quick-witted Spence Rawlson. Whereas Rawlson's movements were fluid and co-ordinated, Bateman's were gangling and awkward. It would, as Lotte feared, be no contest, should Hale Bateman have to face the rancher's son in a gunfight. Bateman just did not have the cut of a gun-handy man. To begin with, the green-as-a-spring-leaf marshal did not wear a gun well. The Colt hung on his hips like some alien growth, completely out of place. The simple fact was that some men were never intended to pack a pistol,

while on others a gun settled like it was part of
them. Spence Rawlson had that kind of gun-
friendly gait. Gunfighters had it. Most lawmen,
too. And if they didn't have it, they soon found out
on their way to boot hill. It was an indefinable
quality that could not be quantified, just
witnessed. The likelihood was, that if Hal
Bateman were to go for the gun he wore in any
speed beyond slow and careful, he'd shoot himself
in the foot.

'I'll see you out, Jack,' Lotte said.

Schofield said, 'See you around, Bateman.'

'Real sorry 'bout bustin' in, Mr Schofield,' the
marshal apologized.

On the porch, Lotte grabbed Schofield's arm.
'You've seen, Jack. Now you understand, don't
you?'

'I do, Lotte.'

'I know you're thinking the same thoughts
every one else in Credence Creek are thinking . . .'

'Am I?'

'Sure, you are.'

'And what would those thoughts be, Lotte?'

'How come I love Hal, who has a marshal's pay,
and is not blessed with the kind of poke and fine
looks Spence Rawlson has.'

Schofield shrugged. 'It's a puzzler, sure enough,
Lotte.'

Lotte laughed. 'Yes, it is. And I'm the most
puzzled of all, Jack Schofield. But it's Hal

Bateman who makes my heart skitter. And it's Spence Rawlson who makes my skin crawl.'

She nailed Schofield with a heart-moving gaze.

'You've got to take the deputy's job, Jack. You've just got to. I saw the way you stood up to Spence Rawlson, and though he put on a show of bravado, he was scared.'

Cornered, Schofield complained, 'There must be someone else around these parts who'll be Hal's deputy. It's a job.' But he knew that most men, though eager for a wage, would not be prepared to back Bateman, figuring that sooner or later, and probably sooner, they'd be stepping into the marshal's shoes in a crisis and facing up to Spence Rawlson, or worse. 'Why did Hal take on the marshal's job to begin with, Lotte?' Schofield asked wearily.

'He kind of inherited the marshal's star.'

'Inherited?'

'Hal's uncle Joe used to be the marshal, until he gutshot himself drawing his six-gun.' Lotte sighed. 'The Batemans aren't the most perfectly assembled fellas, Jack.' Seeing Schofield struggling with his conscience, Lotte pleaded, 'Won't you please think about it, Jack?'

On the promise that he would, Jack Schofield took his leave of Lotte Scott. He strolled along to the livery to get his horse. The moon was playing hide-and-seek with rain-clouds, and Main was an ever-changing mixture of shadow and light. It was

from one of the shadows, in an alley running
between the saloon and the general store, that the
gun flashed.

FIVE

Though handed a dilemma by Lotte Scott which he'd rather not have, Jack Schofield also had the dreary mood he'd come to town with lifted by the singer's bubbly zest for living. He playfully kicked out at a stone, and it was that simple action which changed his course by a hair's-breadth, and saved his life. He felt the painful graze of the bush-whacker's bullet on his left shoulder. But if he had not kicked out at the stone, the bullet would have likely caved in the side of his skull. He dived to the ground as a second flash lit the alley which ran between the Baldy Critter and the general store, and returned the ambusher's fire. There was the sound of running feet from the darkness. One man. Hal Bateman burst from Lotte Scott's house, shooting wildy, more of a danger to Schofield than his ambusher. Just as he was about to give chase to the bushwhacker, Bateman's wayward bullets had him diving back to ground, robbing Schofield of precious seconds in his pursuit of the sneak gunnie.

'Damn it, Hal,' Schofield shouted. 'What kind of twisted shooting is that?'

'Sorry, Mr Schofield,' the gawking marshal apologized. 'My eyes ain't too good, ya see.'

Schofield thought: no surprise in that.

Taking advantage of Jack Schofield's predicament, the alley-shooter grabbed the opportunity to sling more lead Schofield's way. Bullets hit the ground inches from his face. Schofield rolled, and kept rolling as the bushwhacker's slugs chased him, punching holes in the ground. Schofield heard the click of an empty gun-chamber, and took full advantage of the seconds it took the shooter to reload. He sprinted to the edge of the alley, resisting the urge to blast wildly into the darkness in the hope of getting off a lucky shot. Not being a regular gun-user, Schofield did not know how many bullets he had in his six-gun, therefore he had to make each load count. If he ran out of bullets, he would be facing the bushwhacker's reloaded gun, most of whose bullets, Schofield had no doubt, would end up in him.

Hal Bateman was fighting Lotte, as she tried to haul him to the shelter of the general store door. Jack Schofield hoped she succeeded. He had problems enough without having the most inept marshal in the West to contend with.

To Schofield's despair, Bateman slipped Lotte's

hold and came haring along the street. But not for long. A bullet from the inky blackness of the alley caught Hal and spun him around. Lotte screamed. Bateman lay moaning, but not, as far as Schofield could tell, fatally wounded.

Grabbing the split-second opportunity handed him by the bushwhacker's concentration on nailing the marshal, Jack Schofield ducked into the darkness of the alley just in time to see, in a patch of moonlight, the fleeing figure of a man darting from the far end of the alley in to the town's backlots. Schofield loosed off a double round that ripped chunks of wood from the wall of the general store. The ambusher howled. Schofield gave chase as far as the end of the alley, trying to ignore Lotte Scott's screams, but failing to do so. Anyway, he consoled himself, there would not be much chance of finding the ambusher in the gloomy backlots of partially constructed buildings and general debris. He fled quickly back along the alley to Main to check on Hal Bateman, and console Lotte Scott.

By now, responding to Lotte's wailing, men were pouring out of the Baldy Critter, and lights were going on in windows all over town. Doc Witherspoon, in his nightshirt, was hurrying to the marshal's aid, while Lotte, still wailing like an Irish banshee, cradled Hal Bateman's head in her arms. Relieved, Jack Schofield heard Bateman ask croakily:

'Is Schofield all right, Lotte?'

'Yes, Hal. Jack's fine.'

Witherspoon ordered, 'A couple of you fellas help the marshal along to the infirmary. Gently!' he berated the men, as Hal Bateman's moans filled the night. 'The marshal isn't a side of beef to be lugged!'

Lotte fled to Jack Schofield's arms for comfort. Bateman's face was as pale as the full moon, but his spirits seemed to be perky enough.

'Looks like Hal has a couple of busted ribs,' Witherspoon told Lotte. 'Could be much worse. Lucky he's so damn bony. The bullet had no fat to lodge in. Healing should be quick, I reckon.'

With Hal Bateman settled for the night, and sleeping peacefully under Witherspoon's sleeping-potion, Schofield escorted Lotte back to her house.

'You know what, Jack,' Lotte said determinedly. 'As soon as Hal is healed, I'm going to persuade him to leave this town. He just isn't a lawman.'

'Where would you go?'

'East, I reckon. Hal isn't a Western man. He's more suited to clerking or storekeeping than wrangling or marshalling.'

'Maybe Hal doesn't see it that way, Lotte,' Schofield cautioned. 'A man robbed of his pride isn't much good to himself or anyone else.'

Exasperated, Lotte moaned, 'But if I leave him here, he'll be killed for sure, Jack.' Spiritedly, Lotte declared, 'I'll love him to bits. That will see Hal through any pangs.'

'Maybe,' Schofield said, doubtingly.

'Oh, Jack,' Lotte whined. 'What am I to do? Won't you give it some thought, Jack?' she pleaded.

'Sure will, Lotte,' Schofield assured the singer. 'But your problem isn't the kind of predicament that I'm used to solving,' he warned. 'Never was much good on giving advice of the heart kind, Lotte.'

On leaving Lotte, Jack Schofield headed straight for the livery, figuring that now was as good a time as any to haggle with Jess Barrett, the livery owner, about trading his nag for the feisty, midnight-black stallion Barrett had for sale. Schofield was banking on Barrett's being anxious to hit the hay, which might make any haggling with the tough-as-rawhide livery-owner easier.

'Schofield? Jack Schofield?'

Schofield's attention shot to the pitch-black depths of the hotel veranda, where the moonlight had not penetrated. His hand dropped to his gun.

'Easy, mister,' the man drawled. He stepped forward into the moonlight at the edge of the veranda, and held open his coat to show that he was unarmed. The man wore the duds of a gambler, and awakened in Schofield the Western man's natural distrust of the species. His features were hawkish, but Schofield was ready to concede that the moonlight might not be flattering him. 'I don't mean you no harm.' He had the lazy drawl of a Texan.

Schofield relaxed some, but did not entirely drop his guard. A man's body and clothing held a hundred hiding-places. In his experience, a gunless man had often proved to be more dangerous. Some men preferred the stealth of a knife.

'Don't know if what I'm going to say will make much sense—'

'Say it, and we'll find out,' Schofield interjected, his tone discouraging familiarity.

'You're an unfriendly cuss, ain't you,' the man said.

'Careful, I'd say,' Jack Schofield flung back.

'Meant to talk to you earlier in the saloon, before all hell broke loose between you and that giant. Either you're a very brave man, or a hole-in-the-head fool.'

'Make any difference to you?'

'Not one little bit.' He chuckled. 'Guess we're not going to be friends, so... Met this fella called Fred Best in a poker game over in Reeves a couple of days ago. Said if I crossed paths with you here, I was to tell you that he knows Charlie.'

Jack Schofield's heart skipped.

'Make sense?'

'Makes sense,' Schofield confirmed.

'There you have it, Schofield.'

The gambler drifted back into the darkness of the veranda, and the ghostly creak of a porch rocker crept out of the blackness.

'Obliged, mister,' Schofield said, and continued on to the livery.

Dawn was shading the night sky when Jack Schofield arrived back at the farm (still riding his old nag, Jess Barrett having proved tougher if anything about the trade for the stallion), and feeling bad about having refused Lotte Scott's request to back Hal Bateman. He had explained to her that even if he were to become the deputy marshal, he could not spend every second of every day in Hal Bateman's shadow.

'Spence Rawlson will pick his time, Lotte. And it'll likely be a time when I'm not around,' he'd told her.

But there was no persuading Lotte that should he become Hal Bateman's sidekick, the marshal's safety would not be guaranteed. Schofield wholeheartedly agreed with Lotte that Hal Bateman was not suited to Western life, but had failed to come up with a way to get Hal out of Credence Creek and back East with his pride intact. At some point in Hal's life (of which there should be plenty, if he were to die of natural causes, but very little of should he continue to sport a lawman's badge), he would come to realize how unsuited he was for the rough-and-tumble life of the West. However, they agreed, the chances of Hal's getting the time to come to such a conclusion, if he were to keep wearing a marshal's star, were slim indeed.

Jack Schofield was pondering on what seemed an unsolvable dilemma right up to the moment he saw the cabin door made impassable by the coils of barbed wire nailed across it. The cabin's windows, too, had been similarly obstructed. He slid his rifle from its saddle scabbard and prepared to confront the curs who had done the deed, should they still be lurking around. But the morning was absolutely still, except for the sigh of a gentle, pine-scented breeze blowing through the trees to the rear of the cabin.

Schofield soon discovered the full extent of the havoc wrought by the nocturnal visitors. His chickens had had their necks twisted. The pig he was fattening had had his throat slit. The pig's blood was still fluid, which meant that the evil-doers had only recently fled the scene of carnage.

Jack Schofield's anger was as hot as hell's coals. On the battlefields of the Civil War, where he had witnessed terrible atrocities, his anger had never been as intense. He stormed to his horse, vaulted into the saddle, and made fast tracks for the Rawlson ranch, where he figured he would find the foul perpetrators of the slaughter.

Sleepy Rawlson hands watched as Jack Schofield thundered past. The word flashed round Rawlson range that big trouble was brewing. Some men, mostly Spence Rawlson's backers, dogged Schofield's tail right up to the ranch house. A couple cut his path, blocking his way to the front door. One man, who drew iron, suffered a broken shinbone from the fury behind Jack Schofield's boot. The second man, a lumbering giant, had to be persuaded to step aside with a bullet in his shoulder.

Charles Rawlson, angry as Satan having his tail pulled, yanked open the ranch-house door, toting a shotgun.

'Hold it right there, Schofield!' the rancher rapped, and followed his order with a shotgun blast that near singed Schofield's hair as it passed over him. 'I don't know what bug is eating you. But if you're not prepared to discuss it in a civilized manner, you've got two choices.' His stare became steely. 'Get back on board your horse and hit the trail. Or continue your mayhem and get blasted. The decision is yours to make, Schofield.'

Spence Rawlson appeared in the open door behind his father, a sneer fixed on his face. 'You're going to have to stop being so darn reasonable with this sodbuster, Pa,' he advised. He stepped past his father and took up a stance that invited challenge. 'I say there's only one thing to do with a wild animal, Pa. Kill it.'

Observing Spence Rawlson's untidiness of dress, Schofield said, 'Kind of dusty, aren't you? For so early in the morning.'

Spence Rawlson's smirk was a cocky one. 'This is a ranch, Schofield. Ranches have lots of dust.'

Jack Schofield's tone had steel in it. 'I figure

you picked up all that dust on your ride back here after thrashing my place, Rawlson.'

Spence Rawlson glared. 'I told you before that to you that would be Mr Rawlson, sodbuster!'

Charles Rawlson stepped between them.

'What's he talking about, Spence?' he enquired of his son.

Spence Rawlson shrugged. 'He's loco, Pa.'

Rawlson senior returned his attention to Jack Schofield. 'What exactly are you ranting about, Schofield?'

'While I was in town, I figure that your boy and his cronies rode over to my place to have some fun.' His features set in stone, Schofield looked beyond the rancher to Spence Rawlson. 'If killing my chickens and pig can be called fun.'

Outraged, the rancher blurted, 'You're talking about my son, Schofield. What proof do you have?'

That was the flaw in Schofield's case.

'None,' he sighed. 'Other than knowing I'm right in what I say.'

'Then, sir,' Charles Rawlson barked, 'you'd best turn tail. Before I yield to the temptation to kill you.'

Jack Schofield could fully understand Charles Rawlson's rage. He could produce no evidence of Spence Rawlson's crime, and every man wants to believe that his son is not the kind of cruel and black-hearted cur which Schofield was accusing Spence Rawlson of being. Though in his heart the rancher might know the truth of the accuser's words, Charles Rawlson would want his son to be the kind of man he himself was; the kind of man, unless a miracle were to happen, which Spence Rawlson would never be.

Charles Rawlson was a hard-bitten, driven man. But, Jack Schofield reckoned, a fair man, too.

'You want to make something of this, Schofield?' Spence Rawlson's hand hovered over his six-gun in a claw, ready to dive. 'Or are you leaving?'

Seeing a situation fast developing which could lead to bloodshed, Charles Rawlson suggested to Schofield by way of compromise, 'If you have a case to make, Schofield, you should notify the marshal.'

'Yeah.' Spence sniggered, and gave a theatrical shudder, much to everyone's amusement. 'You go tell our tearaway marshal, sodbuster.'

Schofield said, 'Hal Bateman is only a town marshal. He has no say-so on the range. And you know that, Rawlson,' he growled at the rancher.

'Bateman's the only law in these parts,' Rawlson senior flung back. 'Sometimes a US marshal passes through, but the last one was over a year ago. Usually when a US marshal arrives in town it's to use the jail, and he doesn't take kindly to being enlisted in local squabbles. So Bateman's all you've got, Schofield.'

Jack Schofield grated, 'Bateman is in Doc Witherspoon's infirmary.'

Charles Rawlson seemed genuinely shocked by the revelation. Spence Rawlson took the news in his stride, like a man with knowledge of the event would.

'Bushwhacked.'

'Bushwhacked?' Charles Rawlson said angrily. 'Can't abide bushwhackers. A man with a grudge should face up to his opponent fair and square.'

Spence Rawlson shifted uneasily under his father's gaze. The shift in his posture had been barely noticeable, but it was there. Schofield cast his mind back to the rider who had left town the night before, as if Satan had set fire to his tail, when he escorted Lotte Scott to her house. A Rawlson ranch hand, riding to tell Spence Rawlson about Lotte's assignation?

Schofield gambled.

'Guess you didn't like the news about Lotte Scott and me which your ranch hand brought you last night, Spence.'

'News?' Spence Rawlson asked, fighting to couch his question in a tone of languid indifference, but not quite making it. 'Don't know what you're talking about.'

Jack Schofield sighed, and he let his eyes become dreamy, the way a man does after a pleasant experience. He counted on Spence Rawlson's jealous imagination working against him. It did. He sprang from the ranch house porch, snarling like a riled mountain cat. Schofield, ready and expecting, caught the rancher's son with a haymaker on the right side of his head. Spence sailed through the air and crashed to the hard ground with such force that it near knocked him senseless. Schofield stood over him, fists balled, ready, should Spence Rawlson be of a mind to continue his aggression. As he staggered to his feet, Charles Rawlson shoved his son aside.

'Schofield,' the rancher declared, 'you're a whole lot of trouble that needs fixing. I've tried to do things fairly with you, but you buck me at every turn. I've never seen a man so keen on being dead.'

When he spoke, Jack Schofield's tone was as icy as a Yukon winter: 'What needs fixing is Rawlson ambition, sir. I have as much right to sow crops as you have to fatten cows.'

'It isn't yours to plough,' Rawlson senior reminded Schofield harshly.

'It's in my care until I find its rightful owner. Therefore, I have a duty to protect the owner's interests. That's what I aim to do.'

Charles Rawlson warned stonily: 'The Rawlson spread won't stand by for ever, and see its standing diminished.'

'Like I told you yesterday, Rawlson,' Schofield barked, 'you've got water on the north range. Use it.'

'And I told you that the mountains overlooking that range are rich in silver, which I aim to have mined. Mining needs lots of water, and after its done with it, it isn't much good to man or beast.'

Schofield said: 'Then, as I see it, Rawlson, you've got a choice to make. Ranching or mining. You can't have both.'

Spence Rawlson growled, 'You want to bet, sodbuster?'

'If I were you,' Jack Schofield told the rancher as he strode to his horse, 'I'd throw a leash on that boy of yours, before someone'll plant him.'

'You?' Spence Rawlson scoffed. 'Any time you want to try, you just holler, mister.'

Schofield had his leg in the stirrup, when he spotted a familiar figure lurking at the side of the bunkhouse, off to the right of the ranch house. Chancey Grimes. Putting two and two together, Jack Schofield figured that there was a good reason for Grimes's shyness. He took his leg out of the stirrup and hailed Grimes:

'Why don't you join us, Grimes?'

Instantly, Spence Rawlson tensed. 'This isn't a picnic. Chancey's got work to do, Schofield.' He hollered over his shoulder. 'Get to those chores, Chancey. Now!'

Schofield snatched the rifle out of its saddle scabbard. He placed a slug in the bunkhouse wall, an inch from Chancey Grimes's head.

'What the hell was that for?' Spence Rawlson fumed.

'Show yourself, Grimes,' Schofield ordered.

The rancher's son raged, 'You cock that damn rifle again sodbuster, and so help me—'

Charles Rawlson's sternly delivered order spiked his son's tirade. 'Get yourself out here, Grimes.'

'You taking Schofield's side, Pa?' Spence railed. 'Against your own?'

'Grimes isn't mine,' the rancher grated, and added sourly, 'Thank heavens.'

The seconds ticking by, Schofield rasped: 'We're waiting Grimes. Why, you're proving more shy than a bride on her wedding night.'

Chancey Grimes stepped out from the cover of the bunkhouse, his head bowed, tugging the brim of his Stetson low, and edging rather than walking towards Schofield. The beads of perspiration that sprang on Spence Rawlson's forehead pleased Jack Schofield no end. He reckoned that he'd struck the jackpot.

'Let's see you, Grimes,' Schofield said.

'What's all this about?' Charles Rawlson queried.

'I'm betting that Chancey Grimes was the bush-whacker who tried to nail me, and waylaid Hal Bateman, Rawlson.'

The rancher did not comment. Grimes was a man he'd have preferred not to have around. But any time he had thought about paying him off, Spence had made a song and dance about it, and he had backed off in the interests of an easy life.

Sooner or later, he figured, Grimes would tire of the relatively quiet living that the Rawlson ranch and Credence Creek had to offer, and move on to a more boisterous place. He might have done so a time or two, but Spence had always prevailed upon him to stay, when Grimes seemed ready to move on. Charles Rawlson suspected that Spence was topping up Grimes's pay out of his own pocket to keep him around. It pained the rancher that his only son should want to befriend a toerag like Chancey Grimes, when he could have perfectly decent friends in the sons of his neighbours. It worried him too, to the point of sleepless nights, that Grimes's poison would infect Spence Rawlson more than it already had. The rancher cursed the day he had set eyes on Grimes and hired him. At the time he had served a purpose. But now that the Rawlson ranch had expanded as far as it could without bucking its neighbours, a man like Chancey Grimes was a burden whom he could well do without. Almost daily, he had another complaint about Grimes's unsociable behaviour, to add to an already long list of gripes.

'That's a mighty serious accusation, Schofield,' Spence Rawlson chanted, beginning to see a silver lining in the dark cloud which had hung over him only a minute before. 'A man would have the right to clear his name, if you're talking more wind than substance.'

Schofield agreed. 'You're right. If I'm wrong,

Grimes will have his chance to take his pound of flesh.'

'You hear that, Chancey?' the rancher's son hollered.

'I heard, Spence,' Grimes called back, none too confidently it seemed to Schofield.

Spence Rawlson asked his father, 'You agree with Chancey facing up to the sodbuster, if Schofield's accusation is blather, Pa?'

Charles Rawlson nodded in agreement. 'It's fair.'

Spence Rawlson chuckled, shaking his head in wonder. 'You know, sodbuster, you're one dumb son of a bitch. Must be all that pig- and chicken-shit wafting up your nose that's dulled your brain.'

Charles Rawlson rebuked his son. 'Cleanse your tongue, Spence. No call for foulness of speech.'

Spence Rawlson cast his father a sullen, rebellious look. Jack Schofield had seen the look before in men going bad. He felt sorry for the rancher. He had a son who showed no respect, and Rawlson senior seemed not to know what to to about it.

'Let's get this over with,' the rancher said. 'Can't moon about all day. There's a ranch to be run.' He barked: 'Get over here, Grimes.'

Chancey Grimes shuffled forward, stopping short of coming face to face with Schofield. Jack Schofield closed the distance between them, careful to keep an eye on Spence Rawlson as he did so. His edginess had returned as Schofield put Grimes under close scrutiny.

'Well, Schofield?' Charles Rawlson challenged. 'Is this over and done with on your part,' and added, 'If it is, how do you stand, Grimes?'

Schofield had circled the ranch hand a couple of times, in an inch-by-inch scrutiny.

Spence Rawlson chirped, 'I reckon you should make the sodbuster pay for implying that you were a no-good bushwhacker, Chancey. You've got the right.'

'Yeah, sodbuster,' Chancey Grimes crowed cockily, his confidence soaring. 'And I figure it's best that we settle this with guns.'

Charles Rawlson was uneasy with the prospect of gunplay. 'Why not fists, and let it be at that?'

'Chancey's got the right to choose his means, Pa,' Spence said.

'You done sniffin'?' Grimes challenged Schofield.

'Just about,' Schofield drawled.

Having lulled Grimes, Schofield suddenly swept the Stetson from the ranch hand's head to reveal a deep, blood-crusted gouge over his right ear. He spun Grimes around for Charles Rawlson to see for himself the deep and angry furrow through Grimes's fair hair.

'Last night, when I chased the bushwhacker into the alley, I got off a lucky shot that buzzed the wall of the general store,' Schofield explained. 'As splinters flew, a man howled. I say that that man was Chancey Grimes. And I also say, sir, that he got the wound on the side of his skull from one of those splinters.'

Grimes's eyes darted about, seeking Spence Rawlson's help. Schofield counted out any help by levelling his rifle at the rancher's son. Spence Rawlson proved himself to be a fast thinker.

'Why, Chancey got that graze yesterday, when a horse he was breaking threw him against the corral gate, Schofield,' he lied.

Grimes, seeing light at the end of the tunnel, chanted, 'Yeah. That's right.' Snarling, he said, 'And that makes you all wrong, sodbuster.'

Grimes took up a wide-legged stance, his grin evil, sure that he had the beating of Jack Schofield. And Schofield wasn't at all sure that Chancey Grimes hadn't.

'Better step aside, Pa,' Spence Rawlson said, his eyes glowing with pleasure.

Charles Rawlson said wearily, 'What you claim is not true, Spence.'

'Pa!' Spence protested.

The rancher turned to Jack Schofield. 'Grimes spent the whole day repairing the roof of a line shack, Mr Schofield. He was nowhere near the corral.'

Schofield said, 'I appreciate your honesty, sir.' Turning to Grimes, he said, 'We're heading for town, Grimes, and you're heading for jail.'

Cornered, Chancey Grimes whined, 'Spence. I did it for you. To get this sodbuster outa your hair. And Bateman, too. You don't stand a chance with Lotte Scott as long as he's around.'

Recalling the warbler's words of disgust in relation to Spence Rawlson, Jack Schofield said, 'Hal Bateman around or not, Spence doesn't stand a chance with Lotte Scott. So you wasted your lead, Grimes.' Schofield put the ranch hand under threat of his rifle. 'Unbuckle your gunbelt. Get in leather. Ride!'

'Spence,' Chancey Grimes pleaded.

Spence Rawlson turned his back on his former saddle partner. 'I never asked you to do anything like you did, Chancey.'

'Bastard!' Grimes screamed.

'Get him out of here, Schofield,' Charles Rawlson said, mighty pleased with the turn of events which, at long last, was ridding him of Chancey Grimes.

Grimes, out of his mind with desperation and betrayal, grabbed a rock and slung it at Schofield with unerring accuracy. The missile bounced off Jack Schofield's head, stunning him. Grimes's hand dived for his six-gun. He had it clear of leather and cocked when Charles Rawlson's shotgun boomed. At such close quarters, the blunderbuss cut Grimes in half. The shotgun's roar echoed across the range, disturbing the still morning. Charles Rawlson hung his head.

'You had no choice, Rawlson.' Schofield comforted the distraught rancher.

'Yes, I did,' he replied. 'I had the choice of running Grimes off my property a long time ago. I didn't, and I should have.'

'Pa,' Spence Rawlson said, 'this whole thing is Schofield's fault. He's been nothing but trouble since he arrived in this valley. Just like all sodbusters.' He spat.

Charles Rawlson looked woodenly at his son. When he spoke, his voice was quiet and tired. 'Get some hands. Ride over to Schofield's place. Fix what needs fixing.' He turned to Jack Schofield. 'If you'll come inside the house, I'll make good what it costs to replace your chickens and pig.'

Spence Rawlson had a new burst of anger.

'It sickens me that you're kowtowing to this sodbuster, Pa,' he railed.

'I'm not kowtowing.' Rawlson senior glowered. 'I'm putting right the wrong that was visited on Mr Schofield.'

'What if I say it isn't our wrong, Pa?' Spence growled.

The rancher turned and looked unflinchingly at his son, until Spence wilted under his father's blistering gaze. An admission of his wrongdoing was there in his eyes for all to see.

'You do as I told you,' Rawlson instructed Spence.

In Charles Rawlson's study, on the rancher's handing over the amount they had agreed on, Jack Schofield said, 'You know this shindig is not over, don't you, Rawlson?'

The rancher's gaze on Schofield was rock-steady. He agreed: 'I know, Schofield. Not over by a long shot.'

SIX

When Schofield arrived back at the farm, the Rawlson crew were finishing off the chore which Charles Rawlson had set them. Their mood was black. A lot of the men had disliked Chancey Grimes, and would cry no tears for him. Many of them had seen Grimes as a slacker, who had used his friendship with Spence Rawlson to shirk his fair share of the work. Because of his butt-licking, Grimes had enjoyed a lot more free time in town than they had. His fatter poke had also allowed him to enjoy that free time to the full. Still, as cowmen, when it came to him being killed because of a *sodbuster*'s gripe, their loyalties to a man lay with Grimes. Jack Schofield had no doubt that Spence Rawlson would waste no time in making their mood blacker still. The men's feelings were summed up by a one-eyed man whom Jack Schofield had heard referred to in town as Banker Morgan, apparently due to his skill as a poker-player.

74

'We should have burned the place down when we had the chance, Spence.'

Spence Rawlson grinned. 'Well, Banker,' he drawled, 'maybe next time we will.'

Schofield cautioned, 'Any man crossing my boundary with ill-intent won't be leaving standing up.' Widening his address, he added for the benefit of the entire crew, 'Think about that, if you're of a mind to start trouble.'

To a man, sullen faces glared back at Jack Schofield.

Banker Morgan, who was now angling for the comfortable position Chancey Grimes had enjoyed, turned from yanking out the last nail holding the barbed wire in place across the cabin door. He dropped the claw hammer he was working with, and stepped off the porch to face Schofield.

'I don't take kindly to threats from no sodbuster, Schofield.'

Jack Schofield smiled coldly. 'That was no threat, Morgan. That was a promise.'

With a swagger, Morgan turned to Spence Rawlson. 'Want me to kill this sodbuster, Spence?'

It was an offer Morgan knew the rancher's son could not take up without incurring the wrath of his old man. Rawlson senior was getting nearer to meeting his Maker, and like all men who had little need of God when they were hale and hearty, Charles Rawlson was now making up for lost time in the hope that God would look the other way when he arrived at the pearly gates.

However, Banker Morgan had a bowel-curdling moment when Spence Rawlson gave his offer deeper consideration than he had expected. If Rawlson gave him the go-ahead, his bluff would have badly backfired. Banker Morgan suspected that the polished walnut handle of Jack Schofield's .45 had not come from wearing the gun as a fashion accessory.

'Let things be for now, Banker,' Spence Rawlson said. 'Mount up,' he ordered the crew. 'There's Rawlson work to be done, too.'

Out of the Rawlson dust a couple of minutes later, Lotte Scott rode in with urgent news.

'You ever hear of a fella called Benjamin Bottle?'

'Bottle?' Schofield pondered, and then, recognizing Lotte's mistake, corrected, 'You mean Bootle, don't you, Lotte?'

'Bootle? Could be.'

'I've heard of him,' Schofield confirmed.

'He's a gunfighter, isn't he?'

'Yes. Not the top-drawer kind. But he's without conscience, dogged, mean and merciless. Qualities more important than speed in his profession. Bootle will back-shoot a man if he can.'

'He's in town,' Lotte announced. 'Stepped off the stage an hour ago. Met by Clark Baker. Seemed really friendly with Bootle.'

'Clark Baker?'

'Darn, Jack. You should get to town more. Clark Baker is the president of the Silver Bucket Mining Company.' Sighing at Schofield's ignorance, Lotte explained, as if she were a teacher trying to get through to a numbskulled child. 'The mining outfit here to dig out Charles Rawlson's silver.'

Lotte pondered. 'What would Baker want with a gunfighter? A six-gun isn't much use digging for silver. Andy Boyd, the hotel clerk, has got ears that could hear a worm sigh. He told me that he overheard Baker telling Bottle—'

'Bootle,' Schofield corrected.

Annoyed at the interruption to her narrative, Lotte griped, 'Bottle? Bootle? What difference does it make?'

Smiling, Schofield said, 'You were saying, Lotte?'

'Why, you put me right out of my stride, Jack Schofield,' she complained. 'So you have!'

'The hotel clerk was telling you . . .' Schofield prompted.

'Right. Andy says that he heard Clark Baker tell Bootle that he'd be head of security for the Silver Bucket Mining Company. Whatever that means.'

Jack Schofield knew exactly what the fancy title meant. Enforcer. With a capital E. But why would a legitimate mining operation need an enforcer? Security to protect their goods and property, yes. But Benjamin Bootle was the kind of agent employed to dissuade and if necessary dispense with any objectors to the company's ambitions. On first impressions, the Silver Bucket Mining Company did not seem to be the kind of outfit which Charles Rawlson, in Schofield's opinion, would associate himself with.

'How long has Baker been in town?' Schofield enquired of Lotte.

'A week, maybe. He and a crew have been out on the Rawlson property. Why?'

'Well, I'm just thinking that for a mining company president, Clark Baker keeps some mighty strange company in the likes of Benjamin Bootle.'

Lotte Scott agreed. 'What are you thinking, Jack?' she asked, on seeing the furrow of lines creasing Schofield's brow.

Worriedly, he said, 'I'm thinking that Charles Rawlson might be getting into very deep and swift waters, Lotte.'

'None of your concern,' the singer said brusquely. 'Why should you fret about Charles Rawlson's problems, with the grief he's been giving you?'

Jack Schofield opined, 'Charles Rawlson's not a bad *hombre*, Lotte. I figure Spence Rawlson to be the viper in this feud between me and the old man.'

'Spence Rawlson a viper. Now that's a fact!'

'You know,' Schofield said, 'if Spence had kept his nose out of this business, I was ready to cut a path at the end of the south meadow to allow Rawlson's cows to reach water.'

'Why for heaven's sake?' Lotte wailed. 'You think Rawlson would do you any favours?'

'Not Spence, for sure. But from what I hear, Charles Rawlson has helped many of his neighbours through bad times. Heck, Lotte, he's an old man counting down his days. Fretting that what he's slaved to build will be squandered away by a wastrel son. If I'm reading Charles Rawlson right, I figure that if he was in his prime he'd take no lip from Spence. But now he's fearful of a rift between him and his son that will make his eternal rest uneasy. So he's trying to placate Spence, while at the same time trying not to upset his neighbours. Not an easy hand to play, Lotte.'

'Spoiling his neighbours' water doesn't seem the right way to remain on friendly terms with them.'

'That's what's puzzling,' Schofield said. 'Why would a man who has given his entire life to building the finest herd in the county, want to risk losing that herd by mining for silver. A rancher's gold is good grass. And there won't be much of that around, once the silt from that mine poisons the water and range.'

Jack Schofield stated emphatically: 'Above all else, Charles Rawlson is a rancher, Lotte.'

'Where're you going?' Lotte asked, as Schofield vaulted into the saddle.

'To jaw with Rawlson. Put him in the know about the kind of people he's getting in tow with.'

Lotte's anger boiled over. 'I don't understand you at all, Jack Schofield,' she railed. 'You're willing, and even eager to help your enemy. But you won't lift a finger to help Hal Bateman.'

Schofield reined in his horse. Lotte had a strong argument working in her favour, and he admitted as much.

Lotte Scott's blue eyes bored into him. 'So, what's your explanation?' the singer challenged.

'Wearing a badge is not my bailiwick, Lotte. But if Hal gets into the kind of trouble he can't safely deal with, I'll pitch in,' he promised.

'Bless you, Jack Schofield,' Lotte yelped. 'You get down off that horse and I'll hug you like a grizzly.'

Jack Schofield did not oblige. He was only human, and Lotte Scott was a mighty desirable woman. 'I'm not sure what I'll be able to do, Lotte,' he cautioned. 'I'm no gunfighter.'

'But you're gun-handy, aren't you?' she asked, worriedly.

Schofield sighed. 'Lotte, my darling, there's a whole passel of difference between handy and slick, as in Benjamin Bootle.'

'But Hal's got no quarrel with Bootle, Jack.'

'Not yet,' Schofield said sombrely. 'Not yet, Lotte.'

SEVEN

On his way to the Rawlson Ranch, Jack Schofield stopped off at a creek to wash the tiredness from his eyes, and scoop a handful of its sparkling clear water. He wondered how long the water would be sweet, once the silver in the Rawlson hills was dug out. He had seen the poisonous results of mining before, and the wasteland it created.

Schofield could not figure out why Charles Rawlson was opening up the hills. He must know that once the mining started, his ranching days were numbered. Whole swaths of his property would become unfit to ranch. And above all else, Schofield reckoned that Rawlson was a cowman first and foremost.

Jack Schofield's thoughts were interrupted by the crack of a twig being stepped on. His impulse was to draw iron, but he stayed his hand and waited, figuring that if the visitor to the creek had intended mayhem, he would have engaged in it long before he got close enough to make the sound of a snapping twig audible. In a couple of seconds two faces were reflected in the creek's shimmering water. One fancily dressed, the other less so. Benjamin Bootle he recognized from seeing his dial on wanted posters. The more nattily dressed man, Schofield tagged as Clark Baker.

'This is Rawlson range, mister.'

Bootle's words, delivered in a Texas drawl, held not a whiff of Texas friendliness.

'That makes it private property,' Clark Baker added.

'Which,' Jack Schofield replied, scooping up another palm of water, 'makes my being here none of your damn business, gents.'

Bootle tensed, but Clark smiled.

'The man has a point, Benjamin,' Clark said. Then, addressing Schofield, 'But if I were to tell Spence Rawlson that I found you trespassing on Rawlson range, I guess he wouldn't take kindly to your intrusion, Mr . . . Schofield?'

Jack Schofield stood up, turned and faced the two men. 'You're kind of off the beaten track yourselves, aren't you?'

Bootle replied, mean-mouthed: 'We're Rawlson men now. The entire range is ours to wander.'

'Rawlson men?' Jack Schofield scoffed. 'You fellas wouldn't know one end of a cow from the other.'

Clark Baker said, 'There's more to the Rawlson spread than cows, Schofield. We've got our uses.'

Schofield's gaze settled on Bootle. He said stonily, 'I bet you have.'

Bootle took a couple of steps towards Schofield before Baker pulled him up.

'We've got more important things to do than deal with a sodbuster, Benjamin.' The mining chief's smirk was galling. 'Besides, as I understand local relations, Spence Rawlson has Schofield marked for dealing with by himself.' He chuckled. 'Now, the last thing we'd want to do is upset the boss's boy, Benjamin.'

Clark touched the brim of his hat.

'Good day, Schofield.' He strode off, but paused ten paces away. 'By the way, let us have a clear understanding about one thing. Your feud with Charles Rawlson about water is your and his business. Poke your nose into Silver Bucket business and Mr Bootle, in his capacity as chief of Silver Bucket security, will have to come calling on you.'

Clark Baker climbed on board the blue-blood stallion he rode.

'Should you be harbouring any thoughts in that direction, keep in mind that such a call would be mighty unpleasant, Schofield,' he threatened.

Bootle joined Clark. Both men rode out of the creek, glancing back at Schofield and sharing a joke. Schofield checked his anger. He was sensible enough to know that their laughing departure was a taunt which they would like him to respond to, to give Bootle the chance to draw the twin

pearl-handled Colts he sported. That Clark Baker
knew who he was, and of his dispute with
Rawlson, told Schofield that the mining chief had
done his homework well. Which meant that he
was a planner, and planners did not take risks.
Every move that Baker made would be a calcu-
lated one, designed, Schofield had no doubt, to
serve only Clark Baker's ends.

His hackles up, Jack Schofield continued his
trip to see Charles Rawlson.

Hal Bateman's face was crimped by the fierceness
of his scowl. 'What the heck did you go and do that
for, Lotte?' he fumed. 'I can take care of m'self,
woman!'

'Like I told you, Hal. Jack Schofield will only
help out if—'

'If I can't do the job, Lotte. Don't you see—'

'See what?' Lotte interjected impatiently.

'That I'll be the darn fool of Credence Creek,'
Hal whined. 'Having my woman get someone else
to do my law-keeping for me.'

'Every marshal I've ever known had a deputy,
Hal Bateman,' Lotte scolded. 'Why should you be
any different?'

'Schofield won't be no deputy, Lotte. He'll be a
damn knight in shinin' armour! 'Sides, Credence
Creek can't afford a deputy, that's if I needed a
deputy in the first place. The town coffers have
more air than cash in them, Lotte. And with jobs

as scarce as snowflakes in June 'round these parts, there ain't goin' to be taxes to pay me pretty soon, let alone a deputy.'

'Lord,' Lotte groaned, 'give me patience. Jack isn't asking for a wage, Hal. He's doing this for me.'

'Yeah?' Bateman said, suspicion flooding his eyes. 'And I don't like the way you say *Jack* neither, Lotte.'

Exasperated to the point of distraction, the singer exclaimed, 'Don't like the way I say Jack? What way would that be, Hal Bateman?'

His eyes hit the floor of Doc Witherspoon's infirmary. 'You know.'

'I don't.' Lotte Scott lifted Hal's chin and fixed an icy stare on him. 'Well?'

'Kind of soft and warm, I guess.'

Lotte laughed uproariously. 'I'll be . . . You're jealous, Hal Bateman.'

'What if I am,' he said defiantly. 'What man wouldn't be, Lotte. With you moonin' over this fella Schofield.'

'I'm not mooning, Hal.'

'Sounded to me like you were'

'Well, I'm not. Heck, Jack Schofield is old enough to be my pa.'

'So,' Bateman griped. 'Lots of young fillies like older studs.'

'Filly!'

'You know what I mean, Lotte. So don't carry on

like your tail's on fire. Jack Schofield is a hand-some-looking cuss. The kind of charmer who could turn a young fil . . .' Hal cringed under Lotte Scott's glare, 'lady's head,' he corrected.

Lotte, preening and purring like a well-fed cat, jutted her hips in what the marshal considered to be a saloon pose, and said, 'Hal Bateman. What I've got is yours for the sparking and taking. No other man's.'

'Lotte,' Hal whined. 'Darn it woman! Close the infirmary window. Them kind of words shouldn't be passing a lady's lips.'

'Hal Bateman,' Lotte staunchly declared, 'I'm going to kiss you like you've never been kissed before.'

Her pouting lips closed on Hal's and he gasped for breath, but only for a second. After that he was willing to keep kissing Lotte Scott until what little breath he had left ran out.

Arbuckle Witherspoon's gentle cough had Hal scrambling out of Lotte's arms.

'Well, young feller,' Witherspoon chuckled. 'Seems Lotte's medicine is a whole lot better and more potent than any brew I can come up with.'

Lotte slapped her knee and laughed. 'I don't know about that, Doc. I'll have some of what you gave Hal.'

'Lotte,' Hal again whined, 'I swear you've got the soul of a Jezebel!'

Chuckling, Witherspoon withdrew. Instantly,

Lotte bore down on Hal again. Holding his hands up, be said:

'Hold it right there. Another kiss like that and we'll have to have nuptials, Lotte.'

'And what's wrong with that?' she wanted to know. 'Don't you want me as your wife, Hal?'

'Hell, I do, and you know it too.'

'Then . . .' Lotte trapped Hal in a fiery embrace. He slid from her grasp. 'What's the matter? Is Doc Witherspoon's brew wearing off, Hal?'

Hal Bateman's face clouded. 'I can't marry you, Lotte.'

'Can't? Or won't?' she challenged.

'Can't. Not until Spence Rawlson and me sort matters out.'

Lotte Scott wailed, 'Hal, if you marry me, Spence won't have a gripe any more.'

Bateman snorted. 'I figure he'll have more of a gripe than ever. D'ya think just because you'll be carrying my monicker, that Spence Rawlson will lose his yearning for you, Lotte. Darn, girl, that'll only make his longin' for you all the more keen.'

He went on quickly, before Lotte could weave her magic and persuade him away from his sound sense approach.

' 'Sides, Spence Rawlson's cravin' for you ain't the only problem that I'm likely to have to deal with.'

'What other problem is there, Hal?'

'The Rawlsons' dispute with Jack Schofield, of course.'

'But that's not your fight, Hal,' Lotte pleaded, desperate at the thought of Bateman becoming involved in a range war, with all the dangers that such a conflict entailed for even the most accomplished lawman. 'You're a town marshal. What happens out on the range isn't any of your affair.'

Hal Bateman declared proudly, 'I'm the only law 'round these parts, Lotte. 'Ceptin' when a US marshal drops by.'

'A US marshal visits Clancyville pretty often, Hal. Send word. Let him come and deal with the Rawlsons' feud with Jack Schofield,' she pleaded.

Crankily, the inept marshal said, 'Jim Badger never called in no US marshal. Always dealt with local skirmishes. I can do no less, Lotte.'

'Jim Badger,' Lotte reminded Hal harshly, 'was rattler-spit quick with a six-gun. You're not, Hal.'

Jim Badger was two marshals back. Hal Bateman had conveniently forgotten about his Uncle Joe who had been the last marshal, and from whom Hal had taken over after, in true Bateman fashion, his uncle had gutshot himself while drawing his six-gun.

Bateman flinched, and mumbled surlily, 'I'm quick 'nuff.'

'No you're not, Hal,' Lotte said quietly, figuring it was time to call a spade a spade. 'And now that Spence has Benjamin Bootle's services to call on . . .'

There was no need to finish.

'Bootle's not working for the Rawlsons. He's Clark Baker's man. What happens between the Rawlsons and Schofield ain't none of his affair.'

'Baker is working for Charles Rawlson. In my book that means that if Spence Rawlson calls on Bootle's services, Baker isn't going to stand in his way of getting them.'

'Suppose it figures,' Hal conceded glumly.

'Now what chance do you think you'd have going up against a gunnie the calibre of Benjamin Bootle? He's left a trail of dead men behind him, Hal.' Lotte screwed up her eyes. 'Of course . . .'

'Of course, what?'

'If you were partnered by Jack Schofield . . .'

'You reckon Schofield is fast enough to match Bootle?' Hal wondered.

'I'd say that Jack Schofield would be a match for any man he chose to make matching with his business. I've seen that .45 he packs, and that gun hasn't been in any cotton wool, I reckon.'

'He's got the gait, sure enough,' Hal pondered. And then quickly and stubbornly he rejected Lotte's suggestion. 'Lotte, it's about time that you got it through your head that I'm the marshal of this burg.' Lotte's desperation and worry were at a peak, but she held her tongue. She figured that in the coming days Hal Bateman's head would hang low, and she did not want to add to his burden by haranguing him further. It looked like all she could do was pray. If the Lord listened to saloon singers?

Lotte wished that Jim Badger was still around and not in San Francisco, where he'd gone to join the city police force.

As Jack Schofield rode across the lush pastures of the Rawlson spread, he could understand why any man would fight to keep intact the heavenly scented range. He rode through curious cows who paused in their munching to size up the stranger. The breeze curling in from the desert country towards the Mexican border had its heat tempered by a fresher wind blowing off the mountains that would soon lose their beauty to the pockmarks with which mining for silver would deface them. Schofield knew that if he were in Rawlson's place, he'd not harm a shoot of grass or a leaf by having a mining outfit cluttering up and spoiling the design of God's own terrain.

When he reached the hill overlooking the Rawlson ranch house, he was not far down the slope when a rider charged from the yard, rifle at the ready. He sent a slug whizzing over Schofield's head, while keeping up his helter-skelter charge. Schofield drew his own rifle from its scabbard, ready to defend himself should the oncoming rider continue his ill-intent towards him.

Several hands gathered in the ranch house yard, curious to see the outcome of the confrontation. Schofield saw Charles Rawlson come from the house. He gesticulated to the watching men, and several of them began shooting in the air. This outburst of gunfire got the rider's attention, and his headlong gallop dropped to a canter. By the time he reached Schofield, Banker Morgan was ambling, and looking mighty displeased at having his wrangle with Schofield reined in.

'Looks like Mr Rawlson don't want you killed today, Schofield,' he grated.

'Maybe he didn't want to have the cost of burying you, Morgan,' Schofield slung back.

Morgan snarled, 'When Rawlson gives the word, Schofield, I'm goin' to be first in line to kill you.'

A duo of riders despatched by the rancher were arriving now to escort Schofield to the ranch house. On arrival, an angry Charles Rawlson came to meet him.

'What the devil do you think you're playing at, Schofield?' he berated him. 'Riding in when you know you're about as welcome here as a demon in heaven, man!'

Banker Morgan, hogging Jack Schofield's tail within an inch of stepping on it, growled, 'You want me to run him off, Mr Rawlson?'

Rawlson flung back, 'I reckon it would take a lot better man than you are, Morgan, to do that.'

Morgan glared malevolently at the rancher and seemed about to take issue with him, but instead wheeled his horse and rode towards the corral, his anger etched plainly in his stiff-backed mien.

'He's not one you'd want to rile too often, Rawlson,' Jack Schofield warned.

'I'll run the Rawlson ranch my way, Schofield,' the rancher bellowed. 'You just state your business, and be quick about it.'

Nettled by Rawlson's inhospitable reception, Jack Schofield had a mind to turn tail and ride out. He had come on a neighbourly quest to share his thoughts with the rancher about the suitability of Clark Baker and the Silver Bucket Mining Company to be handed the task of mining his silver. Rawlson knew everything there was to know about ranching and cows but, Schofield suspected, very little about dealing with the kind of slippery toad Clark Baker was. His friendliness with, and employment of, Benjamin Bootle indicated as much.

'You going to sit there all the darn day long?' Charles Rawlson asked Schofield irritably.

The urge to leave the rancher to his own fate grew stronger by the second. But though he owed Rawlson no favours, and could sit back and take delight in his ensnarement, Jack Schofield felt honour-bound to alert the rancher to the viper's nest he might be walking into.

'You want your business heard by all?' Schofield asked.

'My business?' Rawlson grunted.

'Yes, sir. Your business,' Schofield stated bluntly.

Charles Rawlson's gaze went to the men hanging about, ears cocked.

'Find some damn thing to do,' he roared. The men scattered. 'Damn layabouts!' His gaze returned to Schofield. 'Best come inside the house, I guess.'

Schofield trailed the rancher to the house. Charles Rawlson was Jack Schofield's senior by all of twenty-five years, he'd reckon, but he put it up to Schofield to keep pace. As he reached the house, he saw the rancher disappear into a room at the end of the long, polished hall. On reaching the room, Schofield found it to be a very comfortable study, shaded and restful. A worried Rawlson was slamming a ledger shut, not liking what he was seeing in it.

'Whiskey?' he invited Schofield.

The farmer nodded his acceptance of the offer. Rawlson went to a decanter and poured two generous drinks into fine crystal glasses. He handed Schofield one, and slumped in the chair behind his desk as if the weight of the world had been placed on his shoulders. He slugged the whiskey, leaving a lot of clear glass behind.

'Well,' he growled, 'what's this business that's mine, Schofield?'

'Clark Baker . . .'

Playing for time, Rawlson took another slug of

his whiskey and rolled it about in his mouth.
Schofield held tough. He did not elaborate further,
letting the rancher pick his own time. At last
Rawlson asked:

'What about Baker?'

'You know his pedigree?'

'Pedigree?'

'Where did you find Clark Baker?'

'I didn't,' Charles Rawlson confessed. 'Spence
did.'

'Where did he find Baker?'

'On a trip to Dodge City.'

Schofield said, 'Dodge isn't exactly bursting at
the seams with mining company presidents,
Rawlson.'

The rancher sprang from his chair. He came
round the desk and stood toe to toe with
Schofield. 'Say what you've got to say,' he barked.

Jack Schofield voiced his thoughts about Clark
Baker as a suitable business partner, finishing: 'I
reckon you'll get your fingers burned, Rawlson.'

'What concern is that of yours?' the rancher
snorted. 'If I lose the shirt off my back, shouldn't
that make you happy, Schofield?'

'No, sir. That would not make me happy. We
have our quarrels, Rawlson, but that doesn't
mean I bear you any ill-will.'

The rancher studied Jack Schofield. 'Sir,' he
said, 'that makes you a very rare breed of man
indeed.' He took Schofield's glass. 'Let me replen-

ish this for you.' As he crossed to the decanter, he invited, 'Sit.'

Taking up the rancher's invitation, Schofield selected a wingback and sat. Rawlson returned with an even more generous whiskey, and sat in the twin of the chair Schofield had chosen. There ensued a long silence in which both men considered the state of their relationship, which had defrosted considerably in the last few minutes.

Charles Rawlson was first to speak, confiding to Schofield, 'Never wanted anything to do with scarring those hills, Schofield.'

'Then why do it?'

'Do you think I'm a wealthy man?' the rancher asked.

Schofield's eyes wandered around the luxuriously furnished room, and then came to rest on the rich liquor in his glass. He said, 'You certainly have the trappings, Rawlson.'

A sudden and desperate weariness gripped the rancher. 'All of this,' he said, his hand waving dementedly about the room, 'is on borrowed time.'

Schofield was shocked. Rawlson explained:

'A series of bad investments back East.' Bitterly he added, 'Paying off Spence's gambling debts, and his damn women, too. And two years ago I lost almost an entire herd to bandits.'

'Bandits?'

Rawlson shrugged. 'An unwise venture. The American price for beef had slumped. The

Mexican army were paying top dollar. I was tempted. Lost an entire herd, just the other side of the Rio Grande.' His shoulders slumped. 'Combined with everything else, the blow was too severe to ranch my way back to what the Rawlson ranch used to be. I'm not a young man, Schofield.'

'So you decided to mine the silver?'

Sadly, he said, 'I have no other choice left to me, Schofield.' He was suddenly angry. 'Ranching is what I do. I'm no miner. Even now, before the Silver Bucket turns one rock, my neighbours are at my throat, claiming that the run-off from the mine will sully the entire valley.'

'They're right to be concerned, Rawlson,' Schofield said. 'It will. I've seen what mining can do to fertile range. A year from now your neighbours will be ready to string you up.'

Hopelessness stalked the rancher's face. 'What else can I do?'

'Does it make any sense to you to destroy what you've spent a lifetime building?' Schofield asked.

The rancher's despair deepened. He stormed to the desk and held up the ledger. 'Every page holds a problem, Schofield. I'm honour-bound to pay my debts. With what's left over, maybe Spence will start again some place else. Not that he's over keen on nursing cows, anyway.'

'Gathered as much,' Schofield drawled. 'He spends more time in the saloon than on the range.'

Rawlson said wearily, 'That's about the size of it, sure enough.'

The dour silence dragged. This time it was Jack Schofield who spoke first.

'Ever thought about asking your neighbours to help out, Rawlson,' he said. 'As I hear it, you've never been stinting in helping them.'

'How can I do that without admitting what kind of a fool I've been?'

'Stupidity carries a price. You're not the first, and you won't be the last man to pay that price, Rawlson.' Schofield settled his gaze on the rancher. 'But pride carries an even higher price, if you let it.'

He let the rancher ponder for a spell.

'Ditching that pride will rip the guts right out of you. You've got to decide if the ranch is worth eating humble pie for.' Jack Schofield stood up, settled the Stetson on his head. 'If you decide to ditch Clark Baker, give me a holler.'

'And if I don't put legs under Baker?'

'Then,' Jack Schofield said solemnly, 'that makes you a neighbour not worth having, or not worth helping, Rawlson.'

The rancher said, 'What if I can have that water and just mine silver for a brief spell?'

'Silver,' Schofield declared uncompromisingly, 'means no water. Sludge will foul what you've got. And that same filth will work its way down the valley, until the range will be home to nothing but bony hollow-siders.' Jack Schofield strode to the study door.

'Your call, Rawlson,' was his departing remark.

EIGHT

Spence Rawlson drew rein in a tumble of boulders when he saw Jack Schofield coming along the trail from the ranch, curious as to what errand he had been on, and more curious still that he was riding across Rawlson range unimpeded. Tempted, the rancher's son slid his rifle from its scabbard, seeing an ideal opportunity to remove a thorn from his side. But he had just come from a meeting with Clark Baker, who had made it clear that gunplay right now was not the wisest thing.

'You don't want anything to come in the way of that hefty payout you're in line for, do you, Spence?' he'd asked.

For sure, he did not.

All he wanted out of the deal was a hefty stake, and an end to punching cows. He preferred a life of gambling and womanizing. With Baker's dollars in his pocket, he planned on heading for Dodge and Tombstone, and maybe on to the gambling-halls, cathouses and opium-dens of San Francisco. He also planned a spell on the Mississipi gambling-boats. He had been charting his future course ever since a government geologist had discovered silver in the Rawlson hills two years previously.

'This range will remain cow country as long as I'm drawing breath,' Charles Rawlson had told Spence in a heated argument. 'And I hope when I'm gone, that'll be the case also. In fact,' the stubborn old fool had gone on, 'I think I'd better make it a condition of your inheriting the ranch that it remains just that, and not some vast ugly hole in the ground.'

Spence Rawlson recalled how he was tempted, when the cranky old cuss had turned his back on him, to settle the matter in his favour there and then. They had paused for a drink of water in a shaded dell, well protected from prying eyes. It would have been easy to convince folk that one of Charles Rawlson's many enemies had ambushed him. He had regretted not acting then, and his regret had grown keener every day until the old man had presented him with a golden opportunity to sink the ranch, and leave him no alternative but to dig out the silver. That was when the old man had decided to sell his beef to the Mexican army. At first the opportunity did not leap out at him, but Clark Baker had readily spotted the chance to put Charles Rawlson over a barrel.

'What if the herd was rustled?' he had asked Spence, on his last visit to Dodge to parley with Baker.

'It would ruin Pa,' Spence had told him.

'Enough to make him think again about that silver?' Baker had asked slyly.

A plan had been quickly strung together. Baker would arrange for a gang to rustle the cattle. Spence Rawlson's part in the plan would be to lead the cows into an agreed canyon, where the bandits, led by Benjamin Bootle, would attack the Rawlson crew. Then, showing consideration for the lives of his men, after a convincing exchange of lead, of course, Spence would withdraw.

Clark Baker had told Spence, 'The scheme will serve two purposes. It will put your pa in dire straits. And the herd will give us start-up capital.'

As Jack Schofield drew near, Spence Rawlson slid further back into cover, fighting the devil's urge to use the rifle. It was a temptation he wished he could yield to, but downing the sodbuster now would bring that fool Hal Bateman on to the range, poking his nose in. He was too dumb to discover anything, but knowing how Lotte Scott felt about Bateman and he about her, she might just persuade him to send to Clancyville for the assistance of a US marshal. It was Spence's definite opinion that should that happen, Clark Baker's dust would be fast and furious. Gents like Baker and Bootle vanished like smoke from a bottle when a US marshal was on the prowl. If such were to happen, his departure for the bright lights would be delayed, if not ditched completely. The ranch might even fold. The thought of having to work for a living sent a shudder through Spence Rawlson.

He put the rifle back in its scabbard.

As Jack Schofield rode past, not ten feet from where Spence Rawlson was lurking, the rancher's son consoled himself with the thought that there would be other opportunities to make Schofield wormbait.

On arriving back at the ranch, Spence made tracks for his father's study where the old man spent most of his days cloistered now, trying to balance books that were well past redemption.

'Pa!'

Spence Rawlson steamed through the study door, straining its hinges.

'Don't you have any manners?' Charles Rawlson snapped. 'It's customary to knock before you charge into a room.'

Spence Rawlson disregarded his father's rebuke.

'What was that maggot Schofield doing here?' he demanded.

'Talking sense,' came Rawlson senior's snappy reply.

'Sense? What kind of sense would that be, Pa?'

'The kind I should have had a long time ago,' the rancher flung back, angered by his son's badgering. 'The kind I'm going to have now.'

'What's on your mind, Pa?' Spence quizzed, his heart-rate picking up, his breath shortening. 'What're you planning on doing?'

'I'm going to ask my neighbours, including Jack Schofield, for a helping hand. That's what I'm planning on doing, Spence. I should have done it a long time ago, before I got involved with Clark Baker and the Silver Bucket Mining Company.'

In his fury, Spence Rawlson almost blurted out that there was no such entity as the Silver Bucket Mining Company. That was just a fancy handle Clark Baker had thought up to put on the fake legal documents he had passed off as his bona fides.

Spence Rawlson's greed had made him blind to Clark Baker's scheming nature. He was unaware of Baker's real intentions to swindle both Rawlsons. Baker's plan was to simply sell the hills to a real mining outfit for a king's ransom. What he knew about mining could be written on a flea's backside, with room to spare. Of course, to do that, Charles and Spence Rawlson could not be around. And that was where Jack Schofield figured. Baker had a slick plan to lure the rancher to Schofield's farm by sending him a bogus invitation. Then, as he rode up, Bootle would ambush Charles Rawlson.

'Spence will go looking for Schofield,' Baker had explained to Bootle. 'I'm betting on Spence being boxed.'

'How will that hand us the silver?' Bootle wanted to know.

Smug as a flea on a dog's rump, Baker said, 'Remember that contract Charles Rawlson signed?'

'Yeah.'

Clark Baker had winked slyly. 'Well, it's not the contract he signed, Benjamin. If you get my drift?'

The gunfighter had smoke coming out of his ears trying to figure out his boss's deviousness. Baker took from his pocket a copy of the contract Charles Rawlson thought he had signed.

He explained:

'Rawlson, the old fool, read every line of the contract I handed him, before adding his signature to mine. I handed Rawlson that contract for safe-keeping. Then I produced my copy of the contract for his signature, which I would keep.' Clark Baker's smile extended from ear to ear. 'Only it wasn't the same contract, Benjamin.' He flourished the document he had taken from his pocket. 'This contract, duly signed by Charles Rawlson, makes me the sole owner of the silver mine. The old fool assumed that he was signing the same contract as he had the first time. But he hadn't.'

Grinning gleefully, Bootle figured he had found

a flaw in his boss's plan.

'Ain't you forgettin' that when the old man is dead, Spence Rawlson will have his contract to challenge yours?'

With the flourish of a conjurer, Clark Baker pulled Charles Rawlson's contract fom his pocket. 'I spun Spence a tall tale about checking an error in the contract that would disadvantage him. He eagerly brought it along for correction.' Baker tore the contract in shreds. 'Duly corrected, Benjamin. That leaves only one contract. Mine.'

The gunfighter had stood in awe of his employer's cleverness.

When Charles Rawlson explained to his son his scheme to save the ranch from going under, Spence Rawlson saw his glitzy future sail right out the window.

'Ain't you got any pride, Pa?' Spence railed. 'Going cap in hand to your neighbours.'

'I reckon they'll be both pleased and relieved that I've abandoned my plan to mine silver,' the rancher opined, and concluded with finality, 'This is cow country, Spence. That's the way it should remain.'

He tetchily swept aside Spence's further protestations.

'I'll go and see Clark Baker tomorrow. Tell him the deal to mine silver is off.'

'He could sue you, Pa. You put your monicker to legal papers.'

Spiritedly, Charles Rawlson declared, 'So be it. But I reckon Baker won't want to stir dust. I figure his past might not stand up to scrutiny. From now on Rawlson range, every blade of grass and drop of water, will be used for what God intended it. Raising beef!'

The panic clamping Spence Rawlson's heart threatened to choke it of life.

'You're going to throw away all that money the mine would bring rolling in?' he argued with his father in desperation.

'This is cow country, Spence,' the rancher said solemnly. 'How could I ever, even for a crazy moment, have thought differently?'

NINE

I can't get a man, who'll take me as I am . . .

A loud cheer and several offers greeted Lotte Scott's plea from the stage of the Baldy Critter saloon. Hal Bateman was sourpussed, as the crowd jostled and pressed forward to crowd up to the stage, and wrapped his arms around his ribs to protect himself from further injury.

Kind sir, won't you take me home with you . . .

The cheer rattled the saloon rafters.

I'll cook and sew . . .

Hal Bateman glowered at the leering, catcalling men around him, hands grabbing for Lotte as she brazenly, in Hal's opinion, strutted to the front of the stage.

Make you howl and glow . . .

Hal fumed. Did she have to crook her finger and beckon so?

Your nights won't be the same, if you take me
    home with you.

The marshal's control snapped when, from out of the crowd and three bottles drunk, Spence Rawlson vaulted on to the stage and grabbed Lotte, his dribbling lips finding hers in the kind of kiss that only women who took customers upstairs got.

'That's right, Spence . . .' Bateman swung around to Banker Morgan behind him. 'Show that tramp what a real man is made of!'

Hal Bateman swung at Morgan, but even without the hampering effect of his injured ribs, Morgan would not be unduly troubled by Hal's attempt at chastisement. He parried easily, and rocked Hal to his roots with a pile-driver.

Lotte screamed. Her nails raked Spence Rawlson's face, and he turned uglier than a cornered polecat.

Bateman's eyes spun with the impact of Banker Morgan's fist. He wobbled like freshly made jelly but, grimly, he remained standing. Morgan's eyes were diamond-bright with the pleasure of what was to come.

Incensed by Lotte's attack on him, Spence

Rawlson grabbed her by the hair and forced her to her knees.

'I'll kill you, Rawl—'

Hal Bateman's threat was cut short by Banker Morgan's second hammer-blow. The gangly-limbed marshal shot across the saloon and crashed heavily against the bar. Imbibers stepped aside to clear a path for Bateman's cartwheeling progress, no one anxious to get on the wrong side of Spence Rawlson's newest bootlicker by lending a hand to stop the marshal's helpless lunge. Past history was littered with men who had been maimed or worse, for crossing Spence Rawlson or his cronies.

Hal Bateman, grimly determined, struggled to his knees. Morgan landed a boot on the side of his head that skittered the marshal's senses. He slumped unconscious to the beer-stained floor. Banker Morgan had his left boot lifted to inflict further punishment, when Jack Schofield stepped in. 'Try me, Morgan!' he invited.

'You're pokin' your nose in where it ain't wanted, Schofield,' Morgan grated. 'That could get a man killed.'

'Hope you're ready to die,' Jack Schofield slung back.

Spence Rawlson, his interest grabbed by the new confrontation, allowed Lotte Scott to escape his clutches. She fled to Hal Bateman's side. 'Whiskey,' she ordered from the barkeep, and held the glass to Hal's lips. Not being a whiskey-drinker, he spluttered and almost choked, but the fiery liquid revived him some. 'Get it down you, Hal,' Lotte pleaded. 'It will ease your pain.'

Bateman pushed Lotte aside and growled at Schofield, 'I can fight my own fights, mister. This is 'tween me and Morgan!'

Banker Morgan grinned evilly. 'Like I said, Schofield. You ain't invited to this shindig.'

Lotte struggled to pull Hal away to the stairs. She had a dressing-room upstairs where he could rest until Doc Witherspoon arrived. She had already dispatched one of the doves to alert Witherspoon. Lotte was losing out to Bateman's headstrong lunge towards Banker Morgan. Jack Schofield stepped in and landed a brain-shaker on the marshal's jaw. Hal folded like a house of cards. Schofield ordered two men to help Lotte get the dead-weight marshal upstairs. They hesitated. Taking up a balled-fist stand, Schofield grated, 'You want the same?' His threat put legs under the reluctant helpers. Schofield returned his attention to Banker Morgan who, by now, had developed a nervous tic near his right eye, a condition brought on by having to deal with a much more formidable opponent in Jack Schofield. His cockiness had drained away.

'You're under arrest for assaulting the marshal,' Schofield told the Rawlson trouble-stirrer.

'Arrest?' Morgan yelped, genuinely surprised by

this twist in the proceedings.

Schofield showed Morgan the deputy's badge pinned to his shirt, and grimly confirmed: 'Arrest!'

Puzzled, Banker Morgan looked to Spence Rawlson for guidance, and was dumbfounded when the rancher's son said:

'I guess you're under arrest, Banker.'

Morgan's eyes glowed with anger at what he clearly saw as a stab in the back. He stepped back from Schofield, pride rattled, his intention clear. 'I'm calling you, Schofield.'

'You sure you want to do that, Morgan?' Schofield asked in a quiet drawl.

Banker Morgan sneered. 'You're a sodbuster. I figure that rig on your hip is just window-dressing, Schofield. To scare old women and boys.' His features set in stone. 'I ain't neither.'

Morgan was hoping his brash bluff would come off, that Schofield would have second thoughts, allowing him to slip out of the bind he'd worked himself into. His earlier thoughts about Jack Schofield's gun not being a fashion accessory, he still believed to be true. Morgan was haunted. How fast was Jack Schofield?

'Now, fellas . . .'

Morgan turned viciously on the woman who had spoken. Cat Lynley ran the bordello side of the Baldy Critter's business.

'Bow out, Cat,' Morgan warned the saloon Madame.

Flinching under Banker Morgan's steely threat, Cat Lynley went back to what she knew best how to do: assuage cantankerous customers. 'If you fellas are hell-bent on gunplay, the one left standing gets to choose a dove for free.'

Morgan said, 'I'll have Lotte Scott, Cat.'

'Lotte ain't a dove,' Cat reminded the Rawlson man.

Morgan chuckled. 'When this is over she will be, like it or not.' He addressed a scowling Spence Rawlson. 'She'll be a present from me to you, Spence.' Now his attention returned to Jack Schofield. 'Ready when you are, mister.'

Banker Morgan called to the barkeep.

'Fill 'em up, Frank. The drinks are on me, boys,' he announced to the crowd.

Frank lined up a string of one-shot glasses along the bar, into which his sidekick began pouring whiskey. The barkeep's action and a hooray from the crowd clearly endorsed Banker Morgan as the winner of the coming gunfight.

Morgan massaged his throat. 'I'm thirsty, Schofield. Let's get this over with.' He called to Rawlson. 'Give us a count of three, Spence.'

Jack Schofield cautioned. 'Don't make the mistake of getting carried away by your own vanity, Morgan. Stupid pride, in these kind of circumstances, has got many a man killed.'

Banker Morgan's eyes were suddenly haunted. 'Stop your blathering, Schofield,' he barked. 'Draw!'

*

Upstairs, Lotte Scott was fretting while she waited for Doc Witherspoon to show. Hal Bateman was pale and gaunt and wheezing like a holed bellows. She had seen men die from less of a head impact than Hal had had. He slipped in and out of consciousness, and when alert he looked at Lotte as if she were a total stranger.

'Hal Bateman,' Lotte scolded him. 'Don't you go dying on me.'

His smile was ghostly, his eyes distant. Lotte hurried to the window to look out on Main. There was no sign of Arbuckle Witherspoon. The doc had a fondness for wine after dinner, often overindulging. Lotte prayed that tonight was not such an occasion.

Hal Bateman groaned and his eyes rolled wildly.

. . . 'Two . . .'

Spence Rawlson maliciously drew out the seconds before he called three. He readied himself to finish what Banker Morgan had started, should Schofield be the man left standing. Every gun duel was one per cent skill and ninety-nine per cent luck. A bad shell, a snagging hammer, were just two of the things he had seen skilled gun-handlers fall prey to.

Killing Jack Schofield was a pleasure he had

wanted to reserve for himself, but events had caught up with him and time was short. His plan to light out with bulging pockets was unravelling fast, after Schofield had urged sainthood on his old man. Best, Spence reckoned, to deal here and now with Schofield. With him out of the way, he might yet have those bulging pockets he had been dreaming of. And once Schofield joined the harp-players, Hal Bateman would join him shortly after. Spence Rawlson's plan of leaving Credence Creek with heavy pockets had another string to its bow, and that was Lotte Scott's company, whether the lady liked it or not.

'Three!' Rawlson called out.

Banker Morgan dived for his gun.

TEN

Banker Morgan's grin froze on his lips. His eyes dazedly watched the trickle of smoke from Jack Schofield's .45. Amazement was the last emotion to register in his eyes, before he fell face forward on to the floor. A hush held sway over the Baldy Critter before, at last, someone murmured:

'Banker's gun never even cleared leather.'

'I'd like to think that this is an end to gunplay, Rawlson,' Schofield said tiredly. 'But I guess it won't be.'

Spence Rawlson shook himself free of the malaise into which Jack Schofield's lightning draw had plunged him. He snarled, 'On that you can bet, sodbuster.'

Schofield, tired of wrangling with Spence Rawlson, was of a mind to offer the rancher's son a chance to conclude their dispute there and then. However, not wanting to add yet another burden to Charles Rawlson's much bent back, he decided

116

against it. It was Schofield's opinion that the rancher had been handed the rough end of the stick when he had been presented with Spence Rawlson as a son, but that fact would not ease the old man's pain should Schofield kill him.

Jack Schofield holstered his pistol, but remained on high alert. Spence Rawlson's eyes were dancing dangerously. He was in a viper mood, caught between options and potentially deadly. All eyes were on him, silently goading him. Spence had lost face, and continued to lose standing as he dithered. His pride could win out. He might still go for his gun.

Lotte Scott's dash downstairs to help the dove whom she had dispatched to fetch the wobbly-legged Arbuckle Witherspoon diverted attention away from Rawlson's and Schofield's stand-off. Jack Schofield gave Rawlson a way out of his predicament by lending his assistance to Lotte, which thankfully Rawlson took, but with a bravado warning to Schofield, which he let pass.

'This ain't over, Schofield.'

'You think the doc, drunk as a skunk, will be much help to Hal?' Jack asked the warbler.

'If he isn't,' she grated, 'I'll kill him myself!'

Arbuckle Witherspoon sat on the edge of the sofa on which Hal Bateman was lying still, unaware of where he was or what he should be doing. Jack Schofield was holding his mouth open, while Lotte poured copious amounts of black coffee down his throat. He gurgled, and the amount of coffee coming back up his throat was equal in measure to the amount Lotte was trying to force into him.

'Steady,' Schofield advised, as Lotte began pouring another cup, 'you'll drown him.'

'If he doesn't make sense soon, I'll . . . I'll . . .' Hal Bateman groaned from deep down inside him. In her frustration, Lotte slapped Whitherspoon across the face. 'Wake up, you old fool!' she screamed.

Schofield took Lotte in his arms and calmed her down. 'Doc's entitled to indulge himself a time or two, Lotte,' he soothed. 'I'm sure that being a sawbones, with all the misery that such a profession entails, sometimes makes Doc want to forget.'

Lotte looked to Bateman with raw anxiety.

'But Hal could slip away, Jack. He's not breathing right.'

Schofield's eyes went beyond Lotte to the washstand in the corner of the room. He hurried over to it and picked up the jug full of water on it. He tested the water, it wasn't as cold as he'd like it to be. He let the medico have the lot right between the eyes. Witherspoon leapt up, reeling, but awake. He looked down at his wet clothes, and then transferred an outraged look to Schofield.

'What the devil do you think you're playing at,

sir!' he berated Jack Schofield.

Arbuckle Witherspoon's tongue still had fur on it, but his eyes were bright and alert. He was on his knees beside Hal Bateman in an instant.

'We've got to get the marshal to the infirmary, and fast,' he declared.

Schofield went to lift Hal, whose thin, lanky frame was not a problem for him to bear.

'No,' Witherspoon objected. 'He needs to be carried on a stretcher, and as still as possible. I don't want his head lolling all over the place.'

'Stretcher?' Lotte said, lost as to how one could be provided.

Jack Schofield acted swiftly. He ripped the room door from its hinges. He yanked the door-knobs from the lock and placed the door on the floor alongside the sofa, and gently eased Hal Bateman on to it.

'Get downstairs,' he ordered Lotte. 'Get a couple of men up here to help.'

Schofield tore a curtain-cord free and secured Hal to the makeshift stretcher. In seconds, Lotte was back with three brawny specimens. Together with Schofield they saw the marshal safely downstairs and across Main to Witherspoon's infirmary where, immediately, Witherspoon began his ministrations, ordering everyone, including Lotte, out of the infirmary.

'Is Hal going to die, Jack?' Lotte pleaded, seeking a reassurance which Schofield could not give her. 'If Hal dies, I'll die too,' she said in a quiet whisper.

'Hal is as tough as old boots,' Schofield consoled her.

She smiled and squeezed his hand in hers. 'No he isn't, Jack,' she said. 'He's gangly and awkward and there's no meat on him. But . . .' her eyes swam in tears, 'I love him. There's no explanation for it that I can come up with. But it's a fact. I love Hal Bateman to bits.'

The night laboured on, until the first fire of dawn showed through Doc Witherspoon's sitting-room window. Exhausted, Lotte had curled up on the sofa, while Jack Schofield rendered what assistance a layman could to Witherspoon. Finally, Witherspoon said:

'I've done all I can do. It's now up to a higher authority to decide Hal Bateman's fate.'

Not a young man, Arbuckle Witherspoon was exhausted. Jack made coffee, but Witherspoon recommended something stiffer, a fine Kentucky rye.

'Have you come any nearer finding who you came looking for?' the sawbones asked.

Schofield told him about the gambler who had passed him word about Fred Best over in Reeves, who thought he might be able to help.

'If this Best fellow doesn't work out, how long are you going to keep looking?'

Schofield shrugged. 'I was reckoning on moving

on pretty soon. Once I have the cabin and farm looking half way respectable.'

'Where are you headed?'

'That soldier mumbled something about San Francisco. Didn't make much sense. He was pretty badly shot up and raving. How the hell I'm suppose to find this Charlie *hombre* in a city as big as San Francisco beats me. If he's even there to start with.'

'That soldier was a lucky man,' Witherspoon opined. 'Most men would have grabbed that farm.' He became thoughtful. 'San Francisco, you say? If you're headed that way, Lotte should be able to give you a few pointers.'

Surprised, Schofield asked, 'Lotte is from San Francisco?'

A low moan from the infirmary got Witherspoon's attention. Hal Bateman was groggily attempting to get out of bed. 'Easy, Hal.' Witherspoon pressed him gently back on the bed. 'Are you seeing me OK?'

Hal's eyes screwed up, trying to focus.

'How many fingers am I holding up?' the medico asked.

He held up three, and just as Hal was about to speak, dropped one.

'Th-thr . . .' Hal stammered, and then changed his mind. 'Two,' he said positively.

'Power of miracles,' Witherspoon said.

Lotte raced through the infirmary door.

Witherspoon blocked her headlong dash to Hal's side. 'Hold up there, Lotte,' he cautioned. 'We don't want you all over Hal, driving his temperature haywire with your smooching.'

'Lotte?' Hal croaked. Then: 'Heck, Doc, step aside. Lotte's the best medicine I can have.'

Chuckling, Arbuckle Witherspoon stepped aside, with the wry comment: 'Right, son. A woman is mighty powerful medicine, sure enough. And I must admit that there's nothing in my medicine cabinet that could come anyway near being as potent as Lotte.'

Schofield and Witherspoon ambled back to the sitting-room, where Schofield collected his hat.

'I'd better make tracks, Doc.'

'You still stringing wire?' Witherspoon enquired.

'Let's say that I've got the wire, if it needs stringing, Doc.'

'That old bull Charles Rawlson seeing sense?'

Schofield opined, 'I think maybe he is at that.'

At the office door, on what seemed a perfect morning, the medico said, 'You know, Schofield, this town needs good men; men of your calibre. You should stick around. Give up on this fruitless search you've been on. Find yourself a wife and settle down here in Credence Creek.'

Arbuckle Witherspoon's crafty eyes twinkled.

'Now, there's the Widow Blayney, for example. . . .'

Amused by Witherspoon's matchmaking, Jack

rejected his offer, and was in the saddle with the medico still chanting the merits of the Widow Blayney, despite his protestations, when Lotte Scott came to the office door.

'You can't leave town now, Jack,' she said. 'Not when the town's needing a marshal.'

'A marshal?' Jack Schofield vigorously shook his head. 'Forget it, Lotte.'

The thought suddenly striking Lotte, she asked, 'Where in tarnation did you get that deputy's badge you're sporting? Hal never said you were his deputy.'

Schofield removed the forgotten star from his shirt. 'I'm not.' He explained: 'Last night I saw Hal going into the Baldy Critter. I knew Spence Rawlson and Banker Morgan were there. I figured Hal might be heading for trouble. So I dropped by the law office, prised open the door, found a star, and headed for the saloon.'

'As it turned out,' Doc Witherspoon said, 'just in the nick of time, too.'

'Get off that horse!' Lotte ordered.

Playing along with Lotte's folksy display of madamery, Jack Schofield slid from the saddle. Lotte's arms instantly entwined him, and her lips kissed his cheek. She said: 'That's a thank-you for helping Hal, Jack.'

Schofield's fingers went to his cheek. His grin was Rio Grande wide. 'I look forward to the next time I can help, Lotte.'

'Bah!' Lotte snorted. 'That, Jack Schofield, is your first and last kiss. Fom now on Hal's the only man who's going to taste my kisses.' She took a couple of paces back. 'Now,' she said brusquely, 'get yourself along to the law office and do some marshalling, Marshal.'

'Hal will be on his feet in no time, Lotte. Won't he, Doc?'

Witherspoon opined, 'A week, maybe a little more.'

Lotte said, 'It isn't a matter of time, Jack. When Hal gets free of Doc's clutches, him and me are taking the first stage out of here.'

'Back to San Francisco?' Witherspoon enquired.

'Yes, sir. Mr Scott, whom I've telegraphed, will fix Hal up with a clerking job in the bank he's president of.'

'Hal's agreed to this course of action?'

The question was Jack Schofield's.

Lotte mumbled, 'Not exactly.' Then, more positively: 'But he will, once I get him to myself.'

Arbuckle Witherspoon chuckled. 'Lotte Scott,' he said, 'when you put your mind to it, gal, I reckon you could make Satan a saint. Now you run along. Hal needs his rest.'

'Walk me home, Jack?' she asked.

'My pleasure, ma'am.'

Before they took their leave of Doc Witherspoon, he took Jack Schofield aside. 'You think about the Widow Blayney,' he urged.

'Mighty fine woman, the widow. You could do worse,' he assured Jack. 'Lots of padding for winter nights, has the widow.'

'Doc,' Schofield's face screwed up, 'if the Widow Blayney is such a darn fine catch, why the hell haven't you grabbed her for yourself?'

Witherspoon paled and shuddered. 'Me? Married? Have pity, man.'

'You know, Doc,' Schofield said with a twinkle of mischief. 'I guess you and me are men who like to taste, but never feast.'

Arbuckle Witherspoon slapped his knee and cut loose with a high-pitched laugh that would have a coyote running for cover. 'Jack Schofield, sir. I guess you've hit the nail on the head.'

'What are you old bulls conniving at?' Lotte wanted to know.

'Madam,' Witherspoon said, with an air of royal haughtiness, 'less of the old bull chatter, if you please!'

Strolling along the boardwalk to Lotte Scott's house in a companionable silence, Jack Schofield began to ponder on Arbuckle Witherspoon's exhortation for him to put down roots in Credence Creek. Maybe, he thought wryly, he should even drop by and have a look at the Widow Blayney. A farm needed a woman; damn it he needed a woman, and by the medico's descripton of the Widow Blayney, she would plough a furrow and master a plough-horse with the next man. If, at some future date, a man called Charlie turned up, he would not hold the soldier to the condition that after five years the farm was his. He would hand it over and find something else to do. But was he a settling man? Was he the marrying kind? Did he want to spend the rest of his days with dirt under his fingernails? There were a lot of questions to answer, and a lot of thinking to do.

Nearing the house, Lotte shrewdly observed, 'Doc give you food for thought, Jack?'

'Yes,' he frankly admitted.

'And. . . ?'

'And I'm giving his advice due consideration.'

'Want to see the Widow Blayney?' Lotte asked impishly. 'Kind of assess her bed-warming potential?'

'How in tarnation did you know—?'

Lotte grinned. 'Doc has set himself up as the Widow Blayney's agent, you might say.' Her smile widened. 'Want to see her, Jack?'

'No!'

But she dragged him along with her anyway. Standing behind an oak outside a pink clapboard house, Jack Schofield watched the Widow Blayney hang out her washing.

'Well,' Lotte asked, 'what do you think, Jack?'

'I think this is a liberty we should not be taking, Lotte Scott. That's what I think.'

The widow bent down to pick up clothes from the wash-basket.

'Is that a glint I see in your eye, Jack?' Lotte teased.

Schofield scowled. 'You've got brass neck, Lotte Scott.' He grabbed her arm. 'Now come on. Before she catches us and lays buckshot in our rear ends. Which we truly deserve.'

On reaching the house, Lotte invited him inside. 'There's a chill in the early air. I've got a bottle of French brandy that will fortify you on the way back home.'

He was slugging the excellent liquor when Lotte tagged on: 'To collect your belongings and come back here to the marshal's office.'

'Dammit, Lotte,' he swore. 'How many times do I have to tell you that I'm not interested in being the marshal of this backwater!'

'Oh, come on, Jack,' she gently rebuked him. 'You've got the look of a settling man about you.' She nudged him on the ribs. 'Particularly since you saw the Widow Blayney bend over.'

Jack Schofield was not a wilting lily, but despite his best efforts a flush of embarrassment flooded his cheeks, much to Lotte's delight. Turning to leave, before his distress encouraged her to get even bolder than she already was, Jack turned quickly to head for the door. In his haste he upended a small table, spilling a photo album on it to the floor, where its pictures scattered. He scooped the pictures up, and paused to look at one of a little girl, not much more than a baby, waving goodbye from a stage window. There was a bearded, rather severe-looking man alongside her. The picture was torn, and the object of the child's attention was missing.

'I was waving goodbye to my pa, I think,' Lotte told Schofield. 'That bearded gent is Mr Scott.'

'The man who adopted you?'

Lotte Scott's eyes were sad and reflective. 'Yes.'

Jack Schofield squinted to read the sign over the stage depot. It read: REEVES STAGE DEPOT.

'Reeves. You're from Reeves, Lotte?'

The singer shrugged. 'Don't know. Mr and Mrs Scott would never talk about my past. They'd say, if I asked, that now I was Charlotte Scott and that was that. My past didn't matter.'

'Why were you adopted by the Scotts?'

'Saul Scott told me that my ma had died of consumption, and my pa could not care for a babby.' Lotte's spirits dipped. 'But, once, when I disobeyed Mr Scott, he got mad and told me that my pa gave me up because I wasn't the boy he wanted. And if that's the case, may he rot in hell!

'But enough about me. Are you going to take the marshal's job, or not?'

'You're jumping the gun, Lotte. Credence Creek has a marshal, until such time as Hal says he wants to hand back his badge.'

A flash of worry showed in Lotte's eyes. 'What if Hal doesn't want to be a clerk, Jack? What if he wants to keep that stupid marshal's job?'

'Would you still marry him if he did?' Jack Schofield asked.

'Reckon I would. Fool that I am.'

'Well, then, my advice to you, Lotte Scott, is that if Hal Bateman means so much to you, you go right along with what he decides. Loving a man for a lifetime will pose enough problems with him sweet. It wouldn't stand a chance in Hades if he's disgruntled by his wife's haranguing.'

'Isn't that just typical of a man,' Lotte pronounced brashly. 'What about the woman being happy?'

Fired by mischief, Jack Schofield said, 'Why, Lotte. Just be glad that a man will have you.'

He just made it out the door, before the plate which Lotte had grabbed from the dresser smashed against it. More plates flew over his head as he niftily made tracks along Main to collect his horse, hitched to the rail outside Witherspoon's office. He had a leg in the stirrup when the office door opened and the doc hailed him:

'Got a moment, Schofield?'

'Hal?' was Schofield's immediate concern.

'The marshal's just fine,' Witherspoon assured him. 'Sleeping like he's just had mother's milk.'

'Then. . . ?'

'If you'd just step inside . . .' Witherspoon invited.

Arbuckle Witherspoon put an arm around

Schofield's shoulders and drew him into the office, where the Widow Blayney sat eyeing him like a tasty meal. Jack tried to back out. However, Witherspoon's hand on his back propelled him further into the office. The door closing behind him had the sound of a prison gate clanging shut.

'This fine-looking lady,' Withespoon boomed, 'is the Widow Blayney, Mr Schofield. Why don't you shake her hand, while I get coffee and cookies.'

Jack Schofield had faced cannon and shot in his time, and had had his moments of fear and dread in doing so. But nothing had terrified him like the woman coming towards him, hand outstretched, smiling like a crocodile, and looking like a rouged coyote.

Jack Schofield concluded that, without a shadow of doubt, the Widow Blayney's rear end was much more presentable than her frontside! Schofield reckoned that her late husband's happiest day was the day he was boxed and finally out of his wife's reach.

A second later, Witherspoon was at the office door, clouded in the dust of Jack Schofield's hoofs as he galloped out of town, throwing anxious back-glances to check if the Widow Blayney was behind him.

'I don't know what got into Jack Schofield just now, Alice, my dear,' Witherspoon said. 'Some urgent business came to mind, I expect.'

'Well, Arbuckle,' the Widow Blayney crooned,

her finger drawing circles in Witherspoon's palm, 'now that we're alone, I'd like you to join me in sharing those cookies you were so kindly providing for Mr Schofield and me.'

Arbuckle Witherspoon, a slow-moving man, seldom perspired. But as the Widow Blayney's muddy eyes lit with a strange fire, and her enormous bosom began to heave as if she had run a mile or two, he was in a positive lather. Doc wished that he had been Jack Schofield's passenger when he'd lit out of town. If he had been, he would not have allowed him to draw rein until they were in Mexico, and even further still!

'Dearest Arbuckle,' the Widow Blayney crooned.

Witherspoon backed away, but the widow kept coming. His backing-off was stopped by a door. The widow had the kind of smile a wolf would have with a free meal in prospect. Witherspoon, uncaring of his surroundings while he had been concentrating on avoiding the Widow Blayney's clutches, found that the door he was backing through was his bedroom door.

Completely misinterpreting his intentions, the widow glowed like a lamp down a mine.

'Bucky, my darling,' she exclaimed, a flush of passion colouring her face to the intensity of hot coals. 'I'm yours!'

Though not a small man, Arbuckle Witherspoon was no match for the mountain of woman coming at him with the pace of an out-of-control train locomotive. He was swept with her on to the bed, and, fine and sturdy a specimen as the canopied bed was, it was not built to withstand the kind of passionate frenzy that the Widow Blayney was in.

As Witherspoon vanished beneath folds of flesh and tossed bedclothes, his muffled pleas held no sway with a woman whose last roll in the hay had been with her husband on that night three years previously, when the widow's passion had shattered a blood vessel in Art Blayney's head. At the time the widow had taken consolation in the fact that her man had died with a smile on his face. No one in Credence Creek had the courage to tell her that Art Blayney's smile was one of relief, not one of contentment.

As the Widow Blayney shed her petticoat, Arbuckle Witherspoon, a knowledgeble medical man who figured that he was beyond shock or suprise, trembled, shuddered, perspired profusely, and prayed. . . .

ELEVEN

Reeves was a town beyond redemption. Most of its buildings were leaning on each other for support, and if one building gave up the ghost, Schofield figured that the entire town would simply fold. Some of the buildings which had been burned in a Confederate raid shortly before the end of the war had never been repaired and stood blackened and decaying. Their rot scented the air and added to the cloak of depression permeating the town and the country approaching it, as its hopelessness reached out to crush any prospect of renewal. Since the end of the war, Jack Schofield had seen many towns like Reeves, the life sucked out of them by the loss of its citizens and post-war depression. Reeves had been, and still was a divided town, part Reb, part Union, still fighting old conflicts and nursing old grudges. It would take time for the wounds to heal. Reeves, Schofield reckoned, did not have that time.

The couple of citizens who were out and about doing what little business there was to be done, suspiciously sized up Jack Schofield. He was used to such receptions. Strangers in Western towns remained strangers until they established their credentials. Then a man was welcomed or shunned, in equal measure.

Lotte Scott's photograph coming to mind, Schofield looked for the stage depot, but there wasn't one. He hitched his horse outside the law office, figuring that would be the best starting point to run Fred Best to ground. He found the door of the sheriff's office bolted, with no sign telling of the lawman's whereabouts and what time he might be due back, as was the norm in small towns where the sheriff had to undertake duties beyond the town limits where no other law operated.

Schofield headed for an old-timer sitting on a creaking rocker on the porch of a decrepit hotel with a faded sign saying: GOLDEN PALACE HOTEL.

The old-timer was whittling wood, and pretending not to be aware of Jack Schofield. But Schofield knew that the old-timer had him eyed from the second he had appeared on the edge of town.

'Howdy, friend,' Schofield greeted. 'What's that you're whittling?'

The rheumy-eyed old man looked up and studied Jack Schofield with his right eye; he didn't have a left eye, just a black hole where it should have been.

'Abe Lincoln,' he said, holding up the image of the late president for Schofield to see. 'Always Abe Lincoln, mister.'

The half-whittled figure held promise. The familar outline was already there, just needing completion.

'It's good, old-timer,' Schofield genuinely complimented.

The old man's single eye frosted over. 'But not your cup of tea, huh?'

'I won't deny it,' Schofield said. 'I'd prefer you to be whittling Robert E. Lee.'

The old-timer continued to consider Schofield, but his hostility slowly faded, and his face returned to kindliness.

'We might have crossed paths,' the old man speculated. 'Who knows?'

'You were in the war?' Schofield asked in surprise. He had to be at least seventy.

The old-timer gave a toothless cackle. 'Lied 'bout my age. Ain't that the recruiting officer didn't give a shit if I was ninety and blind. The day I reported the South had whupped us, and there were a lot of vacancies, mister.'

He smiled slyly. 'That was the one good day the Rebs had.'

Jack Schofield let the old man have his way. He was not in Reeves to refight the war.

'Looking for a fella by the name of Best – Fred Best.'

'Dead,' the old-timer said without trimmings.

'Dead?'

'All them Union cannons deaden your hearin'?' the whittler snorted. Then, added with a disrespectful glee, 'On a bender. Went head first from his wagon.' He spat. 'Deserved, I'd say.'

Schofield did not delve into the reason for the old-timer's hatred of Fred Best. But whatever the reason for his angst, it was, he reckoned, longstanding and poisonous.

'Friend of yours?' the old man enquired, beady-eyed, his hatred finding a new focus for the man who had come seeking Best.

'No.'

'Law?' he asked hopefully.

Jack Schofield shook his head. 'Business.' The old man's face frosted. 'Didn't even know Fred Best existed until a couple of days ago,' Schofield explained. The old man's frostiness eased a touch. 'Best sent word that he might be able to help me find a man I'm looking for.'

'Guess you ain't goin' to be gabbin' now. 'Less you have the ear of the Devil.'

Hopefully, Schofield said, 'Maybe you could help, old-timer?'

'Not with nothin' Fred Best would know, I reckon.' Then, seeing a possible profit, his principled stand slipped. He asked slyly, 'Reward?'

'Not much,' Schofield said.

'What's not much?' the old-timer asked.

Schofield grinned. 'Not much.'

'Tougher than a steer's hide, ain't ya?' the whittler growled. 'This feller you're lookin' for . . . What's his name?'

'Charlie.'

'Charlie? Charlie what?'

Jack Schofield shrugged helplessly.

'That all you got?'

'That's it,' Schofield confirmed.

The old-timer snorted. 'You gotta dime, I gotta dozen, mister.' The old man looked at Jack Schofield as if he'd just found the biggest fool of all time. He said contemptuously: 'You've been a fool, mister. For a bottle, Best would tell ya whatever you wanted to hear.'

He gloated.

'Don't feel bad. You're not the first Reb fool.'

Schofield gave up. It had been a wasted journey. Or had it?

'Got a newspaper in town?' he asked the old-timer.

The old man cackled. 'Newspaper? This town's been dead a long time. Just waitin' to be buried.' His curiosity piqued, he asked. 'Why'd you want the newspaper?'

'I figured that's where I'd find the town's history.'

'I guess.'

Resigned to failure, Schofield strolled away.

'Hold up,' the old-timer called after him. 'I guess the Reeves *Gazette* stuff is in the town's museum.'

Surprised, Schofield asked, 'Museum? Here?'

'Hell, mister,' the old-timer railed. 'Reeves was once a town a man could be proud of! When Sam Waters, the *Gazette*'s owner got shot by a gambler who dealt dirty cards, the rag folded. All its records and stuff were dumped in the museum, 'long with a whole lotta other junk no one needed.'

'Thank you kindly,' Jack Schofield said.

With Schofield beholden, the old-timer pulled a fully whittled image of Abe Lincoln from his coat pocket. 'A dollar.'

Schofield grinned. 'Would that be a Confederate dollar, sir?'

The old man returned Schofield's grin. 'Got all the pipe-lighters I need, mister.'

Jack took a dollar from his vest pocket and handed it over. The old-timer handed him the carving of Abe Lincoln.

'Don't put old Abe in your pants' pocket, young feller,' he advised. 'Being in a Reb's pocket, old Abe is liable to catch fire, and that could burn the only useful thing a Reb's got.'

A burly man coming from the hotel glared at the old-timer. He still wore the uniform jacket of a Confederate major, somewhat tattered and faded, but still worn with pride. 'Stinking old bastard,' the man swore.

Reeves was a place Jack Schofield wanted to shake off the dust of, fast. He tipped his hat to the old man.

'Thank you, old-timer.'

On hearing Jack Schofield's southern tone, the burly man switched his venomous gaze to him.

'The war's over,' Schofield said. 'Let its ghosts rest in peace.'

'It isn't over,' the embittered man flung back. 'Not while there's men like me around to raise the South's standard again.'

The man stormed off, casting back malevolent glances at Schofield.

'You know what?' the old-timer said. 'I ain't goin' to die 'til I sell the major one of my Abe Lincolns.'

Schofield chuckled. 'Then I guess you're going to live a long time, old-timer. Point me in the direction of this . . .' his lips curled in a smile, 'museum.'

'End of Main, turn right. Just bust the door in,' the old man advised. 'Ain't no one there to open it for ya.'

Schofield was half-way down Main when the old-timer called out, 'Heh, mister, remember what I said 'bout not puttin' Abe in your pants' pocket.'

The old man's laugh followed Jack Schofield along the street – the only sign of life there was in Reeves that day, and, Schofield thought, any day.

TWELVE

Clark Baker and Benjamin Bootle were lurking just off the trail leading to Jack Schofield's place. The night before Baker had given a disgruntled Rawlson hand (who had been a friend of Banker Morgan, and took unkindly to Charles Rawlson's statement that Morgan was no loss and would not be mourned), a hundred dollars to pass a message to the old man, saying that Schofield wanted to parley.

Charles Rawlson was eager to accept Jack Schofield's invitation. He had hardly rested since Schofield's visit, giving over every minute to drawing up his plans for the revival of the ranch. He had pocketed his pride, and already had made arrangments to call on his neighbours to lay his cards on the table and ask for their help. He was under no illusions about the difficulties ahead, but had not felt so alive for a long time.

Spence Rawlson, he hoped, would come round. Being his only son, Charles Rawlson might, he was ready to admit, have let too much slide in his rearing of Spence when his mother had passed on ten years previously, anxious as he was to play the dual role of father and mother. His strategy had been a mistake. He had indulged Spence, and in his eagerness to erase the trauma of his mother's sudden death under the wheels of a runaway wagon in town, he had, too many times he now realized, turned a blind eye when he should have stood firm against Spence's tantrums. However, he had now made up his mind to lay it on the line to his son. If he wanted to inherit the ranch, he'd have to put in the work and time to deserve his inheritance. It would be bitter medicine for Spence to swallow, having had free rein, but it was medicine that would have to be taken.

After his visit to Schofield, he would head for town to tell Clark Baker that he had changed his mind about mining for silver. Baker would not like it, and could get ugly. But he would stand firm. The silver was his and it was remaining right where it was, untouched.

'What's keeping that old buzzard?' Bootle complained.

'Probably had to rub in liniment before he started out,' Baker chuckled.

Clark Baker's plan was a simple one. He would bushwhack Charles Rawlson as he rode up to

Schofield's cabin. The Rawlson hand whom he had already bribed to take his message to Rawlson had agreed on another hundred to give false testimony that he was in the vicinity of Schofield's place, had heard the shooting, and had witnessed Schofield lighting out. And with his last breath Charles Rawlson had named Jack Schofield as his murderer.

'What if the marshal steps in to put a leash on Spence when he goes gunning for the sodbuster?' Bootle wanted to know.

'Marshal?' Baker scoffed. 'Hal Bateman can hardly pull his own trousers on without doing himself an injury. Anyway, he's in the infirmary.'

Bootle complimented, 'Your plan is snake-oil smooth, boss.'

'Shrewd planning,' Clark Baker told his henchman, 'is what's kept me above ground all these years.'

On hearing the clomp of hoofs, Bootle craned his long neck to look round the stout pine they were hiding behind.

'Rawlson's here,' he informed Baker.

'You know what you have to do, Benjamin,' Clark said.

The gunfighter slipped his rifle from its scabbard and ran in a crouch to a spot behind the cabin, but above it. He hunkered down, fitting the rifle's butt comfortably against his shoulder. He waited. The plan was to kill Rawlson just as he stepped on to Schofield's porch, to make it look like Jack Schofield had stepped from the cabin on Charles Rawlson's arrival and cut him down where he stood.

Unaware of the treachery he was headed into, Charles Rawlson rode into Schofield's front yard.

'Schofield,' he hailed the house. 'You at home?'

The rancher became aware of the absolute silence. Not even a bird sang to interrupt the eerie stillness.

'Schofield?' he hailed again.

Jack Schofield peered into the gloomy interior of the Reeves museum. Museum was a grand handle for the sprawl of junk he found himself in. The old-timer was right, everyone who had left town must have dumped their rubbish in the museum. Where to even begin to look for the newspaper archives?

'Probably a wild-goose chase anyway,' Schofield murmured, as he began to root through the pile of dusty memorabilia. To his surprise and delight, whoever had stored the records of the Reeves *Gazette*, had been a meticulous man, or maybe a proud one. Figuring that one day Reeves might amount to something again, he had carefully boxed, labelled, and dated the newspaper's records. Not that such attention to detail would help Schofield anyway, because he did not know the date, even the year in which the picture of Lotte

Scott was taken. The archivist's keen sense of duty came to Schofield's rescue. The entire photographic collection of the Reeves *Gazette* was stored in two boxes. It would still be a job to wade through the mountain of photographs, but Schofield decided that he might as well see the hare-brained scheme he had embarked on through. The task took all afternoon and into the night to accomplish. The old-timer from the hotel porch came by with a coal-oil lamp to light the museum's murky interior. The windows, which were not boarded up, had enough grime on them to effect the same result.

'Don't bunk down in the hotel, mister,' the whittler confided. 'Got bugs the size of coyotes.'

'Well, looks like I'll still be here come sun-up,' Schofield said, morosely eyeing the stacks of pictures yet to be searched through. But if he found Lotte's picture with her pa, it would be worth the effort.

'I'll ask Mamie Baldwin to drop a basket by, if you want?' the old man offered.

'That would be fine,' Schofield said.

'And if you're through here afore midnight, Mamie will give you a clean bed to lie in.'

Schofield peeled off a dollar from the small roll of bills he had in his vest pocket, and handed it to the old-timer. Roguishly, the old man examined the dollar bill.

'Not one of them useless Reb bills, is it?' he joked.

He left, his thin shoulders shaking with mirth. Jack Schofield watched him head towards a brightly lit house at the end of the street – Mamie Baldwin's, he supposed.

'You should have no truck with Union scum!'

Schofield's glance went to the burly man puffing on a thick, black cigar, the whiff of which took Schofield back a long way to the tobacco fields of the South: the man wearing the Confederate major's uniform jacket.

'He's an old man,' Jack Schofield said. 'Means no harm.'

'Says the Union had better corporals than Robert E. Lee was a general,' the man said bitterly.

'Like I said,' Schofield said wearily, 'it's time to forget the war, and make what we've got work.'

The cigar-smoker spat, 'It's no-goods and bleeding-hearts like you who done for the South, mister!'

Jack Schofield's fists balled, but he took his own advice. The rancour and bitterness would never cease if every affront brought a like response. He spun around and went back inside the museum.

'You hear me?' the man called after him, itching for a fight.

Schofield ignored the cigar-smoker's gibes until, fearing the anger building inside him, he went and slammed the door shut. It opened a second later.

'Get out of my sight!' Schofield roared.

'As soon as I collect three dollars, mister,' the woman bearing a basket said.

'Sorry, ma'am,' Schofield apologized. 'My bark wasn't intended for you.'

'If I thought it was,' Mamie Baldwin snorted, 'I'd go back to the house, get a gun, come back here and blast your best feature to kingdom come!'

Amused, Jack Schofield asked the buxom blonde woman who, as she entered the circle of mellow light from the coal-oil lamp, quickened his heartbeat: 'Which feature would that be, ma'am?'

Mamie Baldwin laughed. 'Why, the feature that troubles a man most, and whose loss would pain him most, of course.'

Schofield laughed along with her, surprised at the companionable and good-humoured exchanges between them in such a short time. They might have known each other for a long time, so easy in each other's company were they. She set the basket down on a rickety table whose legs were pocked with woodworm, and began to lay out the meal she had packed in the basket.

'Plain and simple,' she said, 'but nourishing.'

Schofield gave her three dollars. She handed him back one.

'Two,' she said. 'The other dollar was by way of compensation for your sharp tone.'

Schofield was not fooled. He had seen Mamie

Baldwin's charitable glance at the small roll of
bills he had produced, and reckoned she had
figured that taking two dollars from such a small
amount was enough. Schofield's pride suffered a
little, but he knew that that was not Mamie
Baldwin's intention. He let it pass, and thanked
her.

'It ain't nothing,' she said brusquely. 'Mosey
'long to the house if you finish here before
midnight. After that, God nor man gets into
Mamie Baldwin's.'

With that she turned and vanished through the
museum door. Schofield went to the door to look
lingeringly after her as she sashayed along the
boardwalk, letting him know that she was all
woman.

Jack Schofield did not doubt it for a second.

A sudden shiver went through Charles Rawlson.
He cast his mind back to the early days in the
valley. There were silences like this one then,
before an Indian attack, when the very air around
a man did not move. Back then they called it a
killers' silence. And it always meant trouble.

Baker, watching from the trees, urged, 'Go
towards the house, you old fool.'

Bootle, too, was willing Rawlson on.

Convinced that there was a threat to him,
Charles Rawlson gently wheeled his horse to
amble back out of the yard. However, after only a

few paces, he spurred the stallion into a full, weaving gallop. Bootle loomed up out of the trees behind the cabin, trying to get a bead on the dodging rancher. Clark Baker played his part by shooting across Rawlson's horse, unnerving and slowing the beast. Benjamin Bootle's rifle cracked. Charles Rawlson clutched at his side and toppled headlong from the stallion. Once free of its load, the horse thundered out of the yard, the scent of fresh blood filling its nostrils.

Clark Baker hurried from the trees. He stood over Rawlson. The rancher half-turned, his pain-filled eyes accusing Baker.

'Sorry, old man,' Baker sneered. 'You're in the way of my becoming a very rich man.'

'Sp-Spence . . . He in on th-this?' Rawlson stammered, a trickle of blood escaping his lips to wriggle down his chin.

'No,' Baker said. 'But he'll be joining you shortly.'

Charles Rawlson's brow furrowed, but he did not have the energy left to ask the question on his lips. Clapping himself on the back for his ingenuity, Clark Baker told the rancher about the clever plan he had set in train to get rid of Spence and him in one swift move.

'Once Spence gets wind of Schofield murdering his old man, he'll come looking for the sodbuster. Schofield will have to defend himself.' He bent down close to the fast-fading rancher. 'On the evidence of how Jack Schofield dispatched Banker Morgan, I reckon that right now Spence is a walking dead man.'

He elaborated: 'With you and Spence playing harps, I get to grab all the silver. Now . . .' Mercilessly, Clark Baker shot Charles Rawlson in the back.

Bootle came running. 'That old man was wilier than we gave him credit for.'

'No problem,' Baker said. He smiled slyly. 'In fact, it's better this way. Nothing gets folk riled more than a man being shot in the back.'

Jack Schofield checked his watch – five to midnight. There was still one stack of photographs to sift through, and he told himself that he might as well finish the task and get it over and done with. That's what he was telling himself, but that was not what he wanted to do. What he wanted to do was amble along to Mamie Baldwin's, and not for the bed and board either. He had spent nights in far worse places than the Reeves museum, but not when there was the kind of homely and pleasurable company on offer that Mamie Baldwin could provide him with.

A minute to midnight, Jack Schofield stopped lying to himself and headed for the Baldwin boarding-house. Mamie answered the door on his first knock as if, Schofield flattered himself, she was waiting for his arrival. She held the lamp aloft, pretending that she did not know who the midnight caller was, but, again, Schofield flattered himself that she knew exactly whose fingers had rapped on her door. Reviewing his assumptions, Jack Schofield thought, amusedly, that he was either in Mamie Baldwin's good books or the biggest fool in Reeves. As he passed inside the pleasantly warm house, with Mamie's scent in his nostrils, he did not care which it was. He was just pleased to be in the company of a woman who had stirred him more than any other woman, in a very long time.

'Come through to the kitchen,' she said.

He followed like a panting puppy. A meal was laid out on the table.

'Sit.'

He was the very essence of obedience. He opined, 'Looks like you were expecting me, Mamie.'

The use of her first name, and in such a familiar way too, earned a sharp glance. In the West, using a woman's first name instead of the more customary *ma'am*, was a liberty not taken without getting permission. However, Mamie Baldwin did not object.

'Eat,' she ordered, but in a way that was more of an impish invitation than a crusty rebuke.

After the meal, Mamie showed Schofield into the parlour and shared the sofa with him. It looked to Jack Schofield that this was not a

woman who stood on ceremony. He was consider-
ing his next move when he saw the far wall of the
parlour festooned with photographs; a potted
history of Reeves and its inhabitants. Mamie was
none too pleased when, mesmerized, Jack leapt off
the sofa and honed in on one particular picture,
that of a young girl leaning out of the stage
window, waving; the exact replica of the picture in
Lotte Scott's album. Only this picture was
complete. Lotte was waving to a younger man
than Schofield had known. But there was no
mistaking the soldier on whose errand Schofield
had come to Credence Creek.

Seeing the object of Schofield's attention,
Mamie Baldwin explained: 'That picture of
Charlotte Armstrong was Fred Best's favourite of
them all . . .'

'Fred Best, you say?' Schofield said.

'Fred was the Reeves *Gazette* photographer.
Stayed right here, up to when he went bad.'

'And Charlotte Armstrong?'

'Ben Armstrong's kid.'

'Armstrong lived here in Reeves?'

'For a spell. Moved over near to Credence Creek
later.' Mamie Baldwin's eyes misted over. She
pointed to the picture which had got Jack
Schofield's interest. 'Saddest thing I've ever seen.
Charlie leaving for San Francisco with those folk
who adopted her.'

Jack Schofield asked excitedly, '*Charlie?*'

'Yes. What bug's got in your pants, Jack? Ben Armstrong wanted a boy. Got a girl. Called Charlotte, Charlie.'

Jack Schofield's mind buzzed. Charlotte – Lotte. Lotte Scott, who was really Charlotte Armstrong, was Ben Armstrong's daughter.

He had found *Charlie*!

'Mamie,' Jack Schofield yelped, and pranced round the parlour with her in his arms. 'You're an angel!'

Mamie said, 'That's the last thing I was planning on being, Jack.'

'That a fact?'

As Mamie Baldwin led him upstairs, Jack Schofield hoped that he would not wake up.

THIRTEEN

At first light Jack Schofield dragged himself out of bed with barely the strength in his legs to hold him up as far as the livery. He welcomed the support of his saddle, and hoped he would be able to stay in it for the journey back to Credence Creek.

'Will you be coming back?' Mamie had asked sleepily as he was leaving.

Coming back? As soon as he could finish his business in Credence Creek, he would turn tail and head back to Reeves as fast as his horse could make it. In Mamie Baldwin, Jack Schofield had found his soulmate.

On reaching the outskirts of Credence Creek, his journey was abruptly ended by a bunch of angry Rawlson hands. The men's leader, a swarthy-faced man, whose Mexican blood showed in every line of his face, blocked Jack Schofield's path.

'Can I do something for you fellas?' Schofield asked.

The men's leader signalled to another man, who immediately removed the lariat from his saddle horn. Swarthy-face looked about him at a selection of trees and picked an oak, over a branch of which the other man slung the rope. He pulled on it to make it taut.

'Get Spence, Bob,' the leader instructed the man nearest to him. 'Wouldn't want him to miss the necktie party.'

Jack Schofield went to react but got a prod of a rifle barrel in his back.

'Drop your gunbelt, Schofield,' Swarthy-face ordered.

Lotte came running, toting a shotgun, which was clearly more danger to herself than to any of Schofield's tormentors. The rope-slinger broke ranks and rode to cut her off, looping an arm around her waist to sweep her on to his horse. The shotgun clattered from her grasp and blasted a hole in the trunk of the hanging tree. The oak shuddered from the impact. The hangman's rope quivered, its noose eager to be filled. The men jeered and cheered as Lotte fought to free herself, while the man enjoyed her bucking attempts to do so.

'Put her down, Seth,' Swarthy-face barked. 'Want Spence to skin you alive?'

'Didn't mean no harm, Diego,' Seth retorted. 'Only innocent fun.'

'Spence won't see it that way,' Diego flung back. 'Let her be, if you don't want to share that noose with Schofield!'

With a wry slant of feature, Jack Schofield enquired of the man called Diego, 'Mind telling me who I'm being hanged for?'

'Don't play dumb!' Diego growled.

'He must be real dumb, Diego,' Seth, the rope-slinger opined. 'To have come back here.'

'Maybe you can clear this mess up, Lotte?' Schofield said.

She did.

'They say you murdered Charles Rawlson, Jack.'

Schofield was stunned.

'See,' Lotte said. 'Jack's innocence of this crime is right there on his dial.'

Diego pondered, but Seth railed:

'I bet he's been workin' on that surprised kisser all night long.'

With the exception of Diego, who was still in a ponderous mood, Seth's opinon was the popular view of the Rawlson bunch. Diego said:

'Never figured you for no fool, Schofield. Neither did Mr Rawlson.'

'You ain't takin' this bastard's side, are ya, Diego?' Seth ranted. 'Randy Barry heard Mr Rawlson bein' shot and saw Schofield lighting out, remember?'

'I remember,' Diego replied testily. 'But Randy's

tongue is pitted from telling lies. And he took off like the wind after putting a noose round Schofield's neck, don't you think?'

'You know why, Diego,' another man said. 'Randy's ma is poorly back in Montana.'

'Poorly, huh?' Diego said. 'Well, she would be I reckon, having come back from the dead.' Stunned faces exchanged glances. Diego explained: 'Randy Barry told me when he first came to the Rawlson ranch that his ma had died when he was a nipper.'

Men were piling out of the Baldy Critter on Spence Rawlson's coat-tails; a baying pack. When Spence reached the hanging tree, he ordered:

'Get the sodbuster's neck in that damn noose!'

He would not accept any reasoned argument from Diego, when he tried to raise doubts about Randy Barry's evidence.

'You're fired, Mex,' he raged. 'And lucky not to be sharing a noose with the sodbuster.'

Eager and willing hands were hauling Jack Schofield to the hanging tree.

'If you hang Jack Schofield on the word of a no-good like Randy Barry, it will be murder pure and simple, Spence Rawlson,' Lotte Scott, whom Schofield now knew to be Lotte Armstrong, warned. 'And I'll make tracks to Clancyville for a US marshal.'

'I couldn't have murdered Rawlson,' Jack Schofield said. 'I wasn't even here. I was over in Reeves, and can prove it.' He told Spence

Rawlson: 'Someone else killed your pa.'

'Yeah? Who?' Spence asked belligerently.

Schofield said, 'I figure the man who stands to lose most if your pa changed his mind about mining that silver. Clark Baker.'

Spence Rawlson's brow furrowed in thought.

'Do you figure that a man like Baker would let a pocket-filler like a silver-mine slip through his fingers? Because that's what was going to happen. The last time I was talking to your pa, I figure he was getting ready to ditch his plan for silver riches, and stick to ranching.'

After his last conversation with his father, Spence Rawlson knew this to be the case.

'Makes sense the way Jack tells it, Spence,' Lotte said.

'Why don't we go and ask Clark Baker about it,' Schofield said. 'That is, if you're quick enough to catch him.'

The sound of galloping hoofs filled the air as Clark Baker and Benjamin Bootle, who had been monitoring events and knew that the game was up, made fast tracks out of town. As the Rawlson hands charged after them, Bootle dropped two of them, sending the remainder scattering for cover.

At the clip Baker and Bootle were going, they would notch up a considerable lead before a posse could be organized. The border was not too far away. The country in between was a patchwork of canyons, ravines and gullies, which made it hard country to track over. Charles Rawlson's killers could easily slip away.

It might have happened that way too, if Hal Bateman had not put in an appearance at the infirmary door, just as the murderous duo were haring past. Hal's six-gun blasted. Bootle slumped in his saddle, and his horse pitched headlong in front of Clark Baker's mount. The collision of animals flung Clark Baker from his horse on to his head. A jagged stone on the road split open his skull.

Benjamin Bootle struggled to one knee, trying to focus his pistol on Hal Bateman. The Credence Creek marshal took no chances. He blasted Bootle again.

Hal Bateman earned many plaudits for his swift action. However, recognizing that he owed more to luck than skill to be alive, Hal finally knew that wearing a star was not for him. When Lotte gently suggested that he should help her with her inheritance long term, he gladly accepted her offer.

Spence Rawlson surprised everyone by the way he wore the mantle of responsibility thrust upon him. Soon the Rawlson Ranch was on its way back to being the best in the territory.

Jack Schofield pinned on the star Hal Bateman had handed in, and Reeves quickly came under his jurisdiction.

Being of a practical nature the good folk of

Credence Creek did not believe in miracles, until the Widow Blayney became Mrs Arbuckle Witherspoon.

Then they believed in miracles.